HAND GRENADE HELEN

THE SCARLET CHRONICLES

LILIANA HART

ALSO BY LILIANA HART

JJ Graves Mystery Series

Dirty Little Secrets

A Dirty Shame

Dirty Rotten Scoundrel

Down and Dirty

Dirty Deeds

Dirty Laundry

Dirty Money

A Dirty Job

Dirty Devil

Playing Dirty

Dirty Martini

Addison Holmes Mystery Series

Whiskey Rebellion

Whiskey Sour

Whiskey For Breakfast

Whiskey, You're The Devil

Whiskey on the Rocks

Whiskey Tango Foxtrot

Whiskey and Gunpowder

Whiskey Lullaby

The Scarlet Chronicles

Bouncing Betty

Hand Grenade Helen

Front Line Francis

The Harley and Davidson Mystery Series

The Farmer's Slaughter

A Tisket a Casket

I Saw Mommy Killing Santa Claus

Get Your Murder Running

Deceased and Desist

Malice in Wonderland

Tequila Mockingbird

Gone With the Sin

Grime and Punishment

Blazing Rattles

A Salt and Battery

Curl Up and Dye

First Comes Death Then Comes Marriage

Box Set 1

Box Set 2

Box Set 3

The Gravediggers

The Darkest Corner

Gone to Dust

Say No More

To Ellie - On to the next chapter in life! I'm so proud of you, and being your mom is a privilege. You've become an incredible young woman, and you astound and amaze me every day.

ACKNOWLEDGMENTS

I could not do what I do without an amazing team and support system helping me. The business of writing has become a family affair, so a huge thanks to Scott, Ava, and Ellie for brainstorming and research. And thanks to Max, Jamie and Graham for the hugs that keep me going.

Thank you to my cover designer, Dar Albert at Wicked Smart Designs for knocking it out of the park with these gorgeous covers. Thanks to my editors, Imogen Howson and Ava Hodge, for always making my books better. And last, but not least, thanks to Scott for being the best partner, husband, sounding board, and all-around "get stuff done" guy. I love you like crazy.

ADA MAE

Present Day

There were those who made it to the end of their days, only to realize they'd squandered the gift of life they'd been given. They had no legacy, no family to speak of, and their bitterness welled up inside of them like soured wine.

For Scarlet Holmes, the word regret wasn't in her vocabulary. Life was meant to be lived, and when things started to free-fall and spiral out of control, it was important to know when to pull the chute before going *splat* into the ground. She'd avoided a lot of *splats* in her lifetime, but she'd had a couple of close calls too—closer than she cared to admit.

The fire crackled in the hearth and the wind howled against the windows—the old panes straining against vicious winter gusts. The sounds reminded her of her childhood, though the house had never been filled with laughter or the smell of freshly baked cookies like it had tonight. Her childhood home had been filled with strife and anger, her father a tyrant obsessed with money, and her mother dissatisfied and obsessed with finding love wherever she could.

It had been far too long since Scarlet had spent a Christmas Eve in Whiskey Bayou. Most of her holidays were spent on cruise ships in a tropical paradise, trying to blot out the memories with mimosas and soft serve ice cream.

But for some reason, Whiskey Bayou had called her home. The more shocking thing was that she'd decided to stay. If she was being honest—and she was when it suited her—this was probably her last trip home, at least on this leg of life's journey. Her bones were tired, and her brain was sharp enough to know that tired bones and a sharp brain brought nothing but misery.

She blew out a sigh and shuffled across the creaky hardwood floor, not sure why she was feeling so maudlin. It was probably the holidays. She'd never liked them much. Holidays were for family, and family had always been in short supply. Her brother had managed to have a son before he'd gone off to war and gotten himself killed, so the Holmes name lived on. And his descendants were as stubborn, ornery, and courageous as he'd ever been.

Scarlet lowered herself into the rocking chair next to the fire and eyed the decanter of whiskey sitting on the round marble within arm's reach. God bless Verna. She'd even put out a clean glass and filled the bucket of ice to the rim.

Verna's mother, Odette, had been the Holmes's housekeeper when Scarlet was a little girl, and she'd asked Verna to take on managing the house after Scarlet's parents and brothers had died. Verna had lived in the house since she was a baby, so it was as much hers as it was Scarlet's, but Verna always made sure everyone was taken care of.

Scarlet poured herself a drink and then looked around at the space that had been the nursery during her childhood. The third-floor rooms had been where she and her brothers had spent most of their youth, and she could still see the yellow-striped wallpaper and identical white iron bed frames lined against the wall.

When the house had been left to her as the only remaining heir, she'd spent part of the fortune she'd inherited removing the constant reminders and memories of what the house had been. She'd updated and renovated and redecorated until it didn't even look like the same house on the inside.

And she'd kept the third-floor suite for herself, having never felt comfortable in her parent's suite on the second floor, where her niece and her husband were currently sleeping.

She'd even added an elevator some fifty years before—the very first home elevator in Whiskey Bayou. Which had been an excellent idea. It turned out climbing three flights of stairs made entertaining gentleman callers difficult, especially when the caller could only carry her to the second landing without having a heart attack.

Scarlet's lips flattened at the memory and she shook her head. They certainly didn't make men like they used to. During the war, every man she knew could have carried her up and down the stairs without breaking a sweat.

The rocker creaked back and forth, her toes only touching the ground enough to set the rocker in motion. And then she stopped moving when she heard the slightest rustle outside her bedroom door. She waited a couple of minutes and then heard the sound again.

"Ada Mae Dempsey," Scarlet called out. "Is that you out there, or is it a big bad burglar?"

The knob turned and the door pushed open, and a pint-sized version of a young Scarlet stood in the doorframe, her pale blue eyes (her father's eyes) wide with a combination of determination and fear. She closed the door behind her and then her shoulders relaxed.

"Did you really think there might be a burglar in the hallway?" Ada asked.

Scarlet shrugged. "You never know. I always thought Christmas Eve was a good time for the burglars to be out. Santa comes in bringing toys, and the burglars follow right behind him and steal it all. I figure that's what happened to most of my toys when I was a kid. My father didn't believe children should play. He believed they should be working, so Santa brought me things like an apron and an adding machine."

Ada squinched her nose and said, "I don't think it's fair to blame getting bad gifts on someone who doesn't exist."

"You don't believe in Santa?" Scarlet asked, shocked.

"It's complicated."

"Come on in here and sit down, girl. There's no point yelling across the room. I'm assuming you don't want to wake anyone up on account of you were supposed to be asleep hours ago?"

Ada pressed her lips together and arched a brow, looking an awful lot like her mother, Addison, in that moment, and she padded across the floor in her slippered feet, wearing her new satin nightgown and robe and clutching a doll in the crook of her arm.

"I suppose if you're going to put it that

way," Ada said, "Then it might be more prudent to settle in and make myself comfortable. Too bad you don't have any hot chocolate."

Scarlet stifled a laugh with a cough. "Hand me that blanket there," she said, pointing to the brightly colored afghan tossed over a footstool. "It's chilly in this old house."

"Daddy says you should get some insulation," Ada said.

Scarlet nodded in agreement. "He's not wrong, but I figure I'll let him take care of it in the next few years. No point in dealing with the inconvenience of construction at my age."

"Is there ever a time?" Ada asked, giving an adult sigh. "Are you getting sick? You should take something for that cough."

"Maybe a little more whiskey," Scarlet said, reaching for the decanter to refill her glass.

Ada Mae crawled into the other rocking chair, and got herself situated with her own afghan and her doll. "Granny says her tolerance for whiskey is a lot higher than her tolerance for people. Did your granny ever say stuff like that?"

"No, my granny always told me to never marry a man who can't shoot a gun."

"How come?" Ada asked.

"I don't know," she said. "In my experience, I've always found it more helpful to be the one who can shoot. Now I want to know why you don't believe in Santa. What's all that about? Aren't you excited to get presents in the morning?"

"Oh, sure," Ada said, waving her hand. "I made a list of everything I want. I even added the websites for an easy shopping experience."

"Very helpful," Scarlet said.

"Daddy said Santa's got it covered, but I didn't correct him. Sometimes it's not respectful to correct adults all the time." Ada quirked her mouth in a way that made Scarlet wonder how many times she'd been given that piece of advice. "But how is Santa supposed to get all those toys to kids all over the world? It doesn't even make sense."

"It was nice of you not to ruin it for your daddy. I think sometimes grownups need Santa more than the kids do."

"Did you ever get anything good for Christmas?" Ada asked.

"I learned early on that it was best to just buy my own gifts. That way I always got exactly what I wanted."

Ada's gaze was serious, and Scarlet often felt that the little girl could see much deeper inside of her than what she deemed comfortable. And if she wasn't mistaken, it looked like pity in Ada's eyes.

"No one has ever gotten you a good present?" she asked.

"Of course I've gotten good presents," Scarlet said. "Tuck that lip back in, girl. No need for a pity party. I've gotten lots of fine jewelry and artwork from husbands and love—umm—suitors —over the years. I even got a gold medal once."

"A gold medal?" Ada asked. "Like the Olympics?"

"Kind of," Scarlet said. "Though it wasn't a gold medal for sports. Unless being a badass counts as a sport."

"You're supposed to watch your language," Ada said. "Mama said to remind you because she's tired of getting phone calls from school on how I'm being influenced."

"Hmm," Scarlet said.

"It's a bunch of tattletales at that school," Ada said, pounding a tiny fist on the arm of the chair. "They can't even let a woman breathe. Bunch of rats."

"I wish I could tell you it gets better with age," Scarlet said. "But it doesn't. You've just got to find the place you belong and the people who understand who you are, and then you'll be able to breathe just fine."

"Maybe you could tell me about how you got your gold medal for being a badass," Ada said.

"Don't push it girly," Scarlet said, tipping her half-empty glass at Ada.

Ada smiled prettily and curled her legs up in the chair.

Scarlet drained her glass and then put it back on the round table, and then she got momentum and propelled herself out of the rocking chair. She was barely tall enough to reach the wooden box sitting on top of the mantel, but her gnarled fingers grasped at the edges and pulled it safely down.

"What's that?" Ada asked, leaning forward.

Scarlet placed the box in Ada's lap and said, "You'll see. Open it up." And then Scarlet went back to her chair, pouring herself another two fingers before she sat back down.

The box opened on metal hinges and the inside was lined with blue velvet. "Wow," Ada said. "That's pretty big. And shiny. Does this mean you won first place?"

Scarlet chuckled. "No, it's not that kind of medal. It means I survived. It's the Congressional Medal of Honor."

"What's that mean?"

"It means that a lot of years ago a bunch of politicians felt bad for not recognizing the roles women played in the war, so they gave us something shiny to placate us."

Ada shook her head and said, "Just like a man."

Scarlet barked out a laugh at that and her

eyes watered with tears. "Lord help the man who ends up as your husband."

"Daddy says that a lot," Ada said. "I'm a handful. I don't think husbands are looking for that."

Scarlet winked. "The right kind of husband is."

"Did you ever find the right kind of husband?"

"Oh, sure," Scarlet said. "I picked a couple of real heroes."

"I'm glad," Ada said, somewhat reprovingly. "Because that last man you told me about who turned out to be a traitor wasn't a good choice."

"No, he wasn't," Scarlet agreed. "But I never would have met my first husband, Pierre, if I hadn't had the experience with Henry Graham. My work with Pierre was part of the reason I got that medal."

"Well, since we both know Santa isn't coming tonight and mama and daddy are probably downstairs trying to figure out how to put that baby walker together, maybe you should tell me about it."

"Maybe I should," Scarlet said.

HAND GRENADE HELEN

November, 1941

The airplane engine sputtered and coughed like a chain smoker gasping his last breaths.

I kept my arms locked around my knees and my head down, learning from previous experience that there'd be a hard jerk once the sputtering stopped, and I was pretty sure I still had a concussion from my head hitting the side of the plane two nights before. The circulation in my legs had been cut off for a couple of hours, and I was starting to regret the cup of coffee I'd drunk to help me stay awake before our departure.

Lise and I were crammed onto the floor of the tiny plane, waiting for the signal that it was our turn to jump. The air was frigid with cold, and my jaw was sore from clenching my teeth together to keep them from chattering. I'd trained for almost a year for this mission—in extreme heat and cold—and there was nothing that was going to keep me from jumping out of this plane.

Well, almost nothing.

It was the third night in a row we'd suited up and taken flight, and hopefully it would be the last. The constant adrenaline followed by let down and disappointment was starting to grate on my nerves. We knew the flights into Germany would be dangerous, but it was the train tunnels they were building under the Owl Mountains near Waldenburg that had drawn the attention of the Special Operations Executive to the small town that rested between the German, Polish, and Czech borders. We didn't know what they were building the tunnels for—not yet—but Waldenburg had become a bustling center of activity because of the location of the train station and the multiple lines that led to Nazi-infested territories so they could get supplies easily.

The problem with parachuting into Germany was the Nazis were like ants, swarming over every available territory and making themselves at home, and our landing zone was limited to a desolate area about eighteen miles from Waldenburg. Our two previous attempts had failed. We'd flown too close to unexpected enemy lines and we'd had to turn back. It was bad enough to parachute into the black of night. It was something altogether different to jump straight into the arms of the enemy.

Lise and I were putting our lives in the hand of our pilot, trusting he could get us to our drop zone undetected and manage to get out himself. These missions were dangerous, and the SOE had lost two planes and their jumpers in the last month.

Even as I had the thought the plane sputtered again and the engine changed pitch as we climbed to a higher altitude.

Howard looked back at us from the pilot seat and said, "Looks like tonight's your lucky night."

There was a groan and a vibration, and the side of the plane opened and the eerie red light above the door turned green. A rush of wind and a few snow flurries whipped through the cabin, and I pulled my goggles down over my eyes and checked the straps of my pack to make sure they were tight. A pack of supplies was strapped to my front, making my uniform bulky and cumbersome on my small frame, but I was grateful for whatever I could take with me into Waldenburg. Believe it or not, jumping out of the plane into complete darkness with the risk of being shot down wasn't the most dangerous part of this operation.

I looked at Lise and she nodded, and then we both tried to beat some feeling back into our legs as we scooted our way over to the opening.

Howard looked back at us and gave the thumbs up, and I watched as Lise gave the sign of the cross and then disappeared into the night air. I had no time to think or say a prayer. I followed right after her. The last thing we wanted was to get separated because we hadn't jumped close enough together.

I'd done the jumps during training, but there was nothing quite like the real thing. The exhilaration of falling into the abyss of the unknown, the wind slapping against my face, and my heart thumping so fast I was afraid it would leap out of my chest before I had the chance to pull the chute was better than sex.

I'd been counting in my head and pulled the string on my chute, and my body jerked as the olive-green nylon caught wind and the freefall stopped. I couldn't see Lise, but I knew she was there. Our training was embedded and we each had our own mission. Shapes of darkness approached, and I said a quick prayer as the ground grew closer. Jumping was the easy part. Landing was harder.

The dark shapes started taking form as I got

closer to the ground, and the fir trees seemed impossibly close together with no room for me to squeeze between them. But I didn't have a choice, and I straightened my arms and legs so I was like an arrow shooting between the firs. There was more room than I'd realized and my body swayed as the parachute floated me into a wooded wonderland. I held my breath and waited for the parachute to clear the trees. The last thing I wanted was to be held hostage by my own parachute and wait for the Nazis to find me hanging from a tree.

The smell of fresh pine and earth would be embedded in my senses forever. I bent my knees, leaned back, and braced myself for impact and my feet skidded across pine needles and soft dirt. I came to a stop on my bottom, but I didn't stay sitting. I jumped up and gathered my parachute, shoving it back in the pack as quickly as I could, and then I snapped a couple of the lower hanging fir branches and scraped them across the area where I'd landed, covering my tracks.

My heart pounded in my ears, and I tried to hear any other movement stirring in the woods, but I wasn't sure I would have been able to in that moment. A twig snapped behind me and I whirled around to see Lise. She was a tall woman with dark hair and dark eyes, and her chute was already packed away.

We had different missions and were going in different directions, but we'd gotten to be friends during our training, and we both knew this could be the last time we saw each other. But there were some things that were bigger than our own lives, and this war was one of them. We hugged each other quickly, and then she turned away and headed in the other direction.

I was alone. And I had a long way to go before I'd come across my contact. I unzipped the pack on my front and got out a small pen light and my compass, and then I zipped the bag closed.

I was careful in how I pointed the light—only to check the time on my watch and to make sure I was heading in a southwest direction toward Waldenburg. I was behind schedule. We'd spent too much time in the air before we'd come to the drop spot, and if I didn't get to my contact within the window of time, I'd have to hide in the woods until I could meet him again the next night.

Even as I had the thought the snow flurries increased. I definitely didn't want to have to camp out. I started moving toward Waldenburg, calculating in my head how many hours it would take me before I reached the designated meeting point. If I didn't stop, and I kept a steady pace, I could do it in just a few hours. And a few hours would put me right at the window of rendezvous.

I prayed for endurance and moved as fast as I could keep quiet. I would beat the time needed, and Pierre Lavigne would come face to face with Hand Grenade Helen before sunrise, or I'd die trying.

DOUBLOON

My heels were blistered after the eighteen-mile trek toward the town center, and every step I took was excruciating. The stockings inside my boots were wet with blood, but the pain kept my mind off the cold and increasing snow flurries.

A soft yellow glow covered the city like a halo, so it was visible from the tree cover, and I wondered if they'd lit lamps or if parts of the city were on fire like I'd witnessed in Marseille. But there was no accompanying smoke, so I could only assume it was something out of the ordinary. Even the gas for lanterns was strictly rationed. I couldn't imagine an entire town ignoring the mandate.

My movements were sluggish and increasingly uncoordinated as I traversed the uneven terrain. My heart pounded loudly in my chest and my breath came in great gasps, so the crack of a branch snapping nearby barely registered.

My feet were like leaden weights, and I stumbled as I moved to get low and hide behind the nearest tree. I pressed my back against the rough bark and pulled the small knife from the sheath in my boot. And then I listened.

There was nothing but the sound of my own panting breath, and I licked my lips together and tried to pucker my mouth so I could give the coded whistle—if the intruder was an ally he'd whistle back—if not, the knife in my hand would have to strike quickly. But it was all for naught because I couldn't make any sound. My mouth was dry and sucking in oxygen wouldn't allow me to even form the shape needed. It wouldn't have mattered anyway, the pitched bird call I'd failed to attempt sounded just behind my left shoulder, and then a hand came across my mouth and a sharp blade pressed against the tender skin of my neck. My pulse pounded beneath the knife.

"You are so loud I'm surprised the entire Nazi army isn't here to greet you," whispered a voice in my ear. French rolled easily off his tongue. "I could hear you coming for the last mile."

"Next time, maybe you could be a gentleman and give me a piggyback," I returned in French. "Blood is hell to get out of stockings."

"Give me the code word or you die here," he said.

"Doubloon," I said. "You are Pierre?"

He removed the knife from my throat and moved in front of me. "Americans," he said in heavily accented English. He knelt and worked at the laces on my boots. "I am Peter for this mission. And you are Helen."

"For now," I said.

"I know your real name. I've read your file. It's why I selected you. Though now that I see you in person I'm not sure you'll do at all."

"Charming," I said. "Unfortunately, they didn't give me any background on you. I can see why."

His chuckle was low as he tried to pull the first boot from my heel.

"I can walk," I hissed, swatting his hands away. "If you take them off I'm likely to never get them back on again."

"Doesn't matter," he said. "I've got your travel clothing with me. It'll be light soon, and we've only got a little over an hour until the first train arrives at the station. Have you been briefed?"

"I was given the coordinates to meet my contact, and a supply pack for the mission. I was told you would fill me in."

"You don't trust me," he said.

"No," I told him.

A small grin etched across his face—in fact, I realized I could see his entire face. Between the brightness of the snow, the moonlight, and the unusual glow coming from the town, we would both be plainly visible to anyone patrolling the area.

"You are wise not to trust me," he said. "I do not trust you either. But we will do our jobs and possibly die. And then only God knows what side we stand on in the end."

I held back a groan as he finally worked the boot from my foot, and he hissed as he tried to remove the stocking. The blood had dried around the wounds, and he pulled a canteen from his belt and poured water over the area until the stocking loosened and came free.

"We need to move," I said. "We are too visible here."

"We are fine for now," he said. "Last night was the celebration of Saint Martin's Festival. Most of the soldiers are passed out in their beds or in the tavern. The lanterns are still lit in town. There is an exception for rations on holidays. This was a good time to arrive. Drink." He shoved the canteen into my hands and then shrugged the pack from his shoulders.

I took slow sips and watched him carefully. He was right that I didn't trust him. My time in Marseille had taught me a valuable lesson—that even those who seemed to be on the side of good could be tempted by evil.

The people in this region had a specific look about them, which was why I'd been told I was a good fit for this particular mission. It was news to me that Pierre had gotten to choose me specifically, but if he was in charge he'd know exactly what he needed better than anyone else.

I was taller than the average woman, and my face had a slightly exotic quality to it—high cheek bones, a straight nose, and almond-shaped gray eyes. I noticed that Pierre had similar features, though his hair was shades lighter than my own.

"Here," he said. "Let's take care of your feet as best we can and then you need to get changed as quickly as possible."

He patted me down rather rudely, but it wasn't sexual in nature. I assumed he was trying to get a better idea of what he was dealing with, and I considered myself right when he found the latch for the pack around my waist and unclasped it.

"I'll hold onto these," he said. "It's best you don't get caught with these components on your person."

"Am I about to be in danger of getting caught?" I asked, shrugging out of my para-chute pack and tugging at the buttons on my jumpsuit. He wiped some salve on the raw places on my feet and put a thin layer of gauze on top.

"Most definitely," he said.

"I wasn't briefed on my role. I've got no cover story. No background. I was told I needed to blend with the people while I'm here, but that most of my talents would be in the field. I know there are detonation devices in the pack you're holding. I'm exceptional at explosives."

"I don't believe you'll ever blend in with the people," he said. "Your features are much too noticeable. There wasn't a photograph in your file. I don't think I'd have selected you if there had been."

It was the first time anyone had ever commented on my looks as if they were a bad thing, especially when it was a man doing the commenting.

"I was briefed on your abilities the last time I was in London," he said. "Your intelligence and skill with languages won't make this a difficult assignment. And yes, your talents, and mine too, will mostly be utilized in the field. But for now, we need to go to the train station."

"And what are we going to the train station for?" I asked, shimmying out of my jumpsuit.

Pierre matter-of-factly took neatly folded clothes out of a canvas bag I hadn't noticed, and he handed me undergarments and winter stockings, waiting patiently for me to put them on before he shook out a herringbone traveling suit and a black swing coat.

Goosebumps pebbled all over my body and I looked at the heeled shoes with trepidation as he set them in front of me. He handed me a pair of black leather gloves and a stylish charcoal hat.

"Shake out your hair," he commanded, handing me a brush. "You've got twigs and fir needles sticking out."

I brushed my hair until it crackled and then I poured some of the water from the canteen into my hands and smoothed it some. I poured more and then scrubbed my face clean. I could tell by looking that all the clothing was French and finely made, but there was wear on the buttons and some of the seams. The SOE saw to every detail. It was rare for brand new clothes to be worn because of rations, so wearing something that looked like it had never been worn was like waving a red flag in the air.

"You haven't answered my question," I said after several minutes had passed. "Why are we going to the train station?"

He turned and inspected me from head to toe, and then he nodded, though he still looked bothered by my appearance.

"We're going to collect my wife," he finally said. "I hope you can walk in those shoes."

THE TRAIN STATION

I decided I was better off in my stocking feet rather than attempting to put the shoes on for the mile trek to the station. The stockings would be ruined, but hopefully no one would be examining my feet anyway, or they'd have more questions than just about ruined stockings.

I carried my hat in hand, and I watched curiously as Pierre slung the parachute pack high up into one of the towering firs, where it caught hold on one of the branches. His aim had been true. It was almost impossible to see it unless you knew where and what to look for.

Another fifty paces or so, he buried the canvas bag that held my old clothing and the supply pack I'd brought with me under a pile of dead leaves, covering the disturbance easily and then breaking off several low-hanging fir branches and placing them on top of the leaves.

It would make it easily identifiable when he came back to retrieve them.

I kept my hand on his shoulder to keep our movements minimal and in sync as he led us to where we were going. He carried a small suitcase and I wondered if his own traveling clothes were inside. He still wore the dark clothes of someone who was trying to disappear, and I had an uneasy feeling I couldn't explain. The SOE might have designated Pierre Lavigne as a top asset and agent, but they'd been wrong before.

"What do you mean we'll be collecting your wife?" I whispered, halfway into our journey.

"I wondered how long it would take you to ask," he said. I could hear the smile in his voice. "Women are all the same. Jealous creatures by nature."

I laughed softly. "That's interesting psychology. My assumption would be that your "wife" is also a spy. Which means I now have two people to distrust instead of just one. But we can call that jealousy if it makes you feel better. I'll still kill you both if you are working for the enemy."

He didn't turn back to look at me, but I could feel his shoulder tense beneath my hand. "Your mission in Marseille burned you badly. But all agents, at least the ones who are good at their jobs, have had an experience like yours. You either die or you come away better at the job. You've come away better. Now you must decide not *who* you trust, but *how* you trust. Because there will be times when you have no choice but to put your life in someone else's hands."

I knew he spoke the truth, but it didn't mean I had to like it.

"As far as you're concerned," he said. "For this mission, *you* will be my wife."

"Lucky me," I said sweetly.

"It seems you've grown claws since Marseille," he said.

"They've always been there. Marseille just sharpened them. It seems the SOE has been thorough in my file."

"Yes," he said, and left it at that. "Now, listen closely. We are the Beauchamps. Peter and Helen. French citizens living in Waldenburg. Our paperwork has been forged and is accurate. The SOE has had me in place here for almost a year. I own a French stationary shop just off *A.H. Strasse*. You've been in Switzerland for the last four months taking care of your ailing mother who moved there for the hot springs, in hopes it would help with her health. She's recently passed, so you're coming back home to your adoring husband, who is somewhat of a scoundrel, but well liked in Waldenburg."

I wouldn't forget our cover story. I not only had a photographic memory, but I could recall any conversation I've ever had with near perfect accuracy. And Pierre had been right about my language skills. The last year of intensive SOE training had focused on my God given talents, something that had only been used for my father's criminal activities up to this point in life.

Waldenburg was technically in the northern province of Germany, but it was close to the Polish, and the elite French who were trying to stay neutral in the war or bribe their way out of harm's way could be found in plentiful numbers in these border towns. There was a healthy mix of nationalities. I spoke German like a native, and I could more than hold my own in Polish, but I was as comfortable with French now as I'd ever been with English.

"How long have the Nazi's been using this as a base?" I asked.

"Only three months," he said. "As they've expanded their territory they're moving into locations that will give them strategic advantage for supplies and transport. Fortunately, the SOE foresaw that and has had people in place ahead of time to get established. The train station in Waldenburg is a crossing station—it has multiple tracks and routes and multiple platforms—and everything from people to goods to coal and minerals go in and out of this station on a regular basis from sun up to sun down. There is always a crowd because it services every surrounding city in Germany, Poland, and Czechia.

"Hitler has made his presence known here. Travel restrictions are being implemented and the number of guards increases weekly. They've started building barbed-wire fences for as far as the eye can see. But they haven't finished yet. Which is to our advantage."

"There are rumors the Nazis are building tunnels under the mountain itself," I said.

"Another reason why this train station has become a rather important stopping point," he said. "But the tunnels under the mountain aren't our mission. At least not yet. I've got to reintroduce you to Waldenburg as my wife. Everyone knows you've been away for months visiting your mother, and before that you were still in France, overseeing our move here. This is a critical moment for everyone who knows who I am in this area.

"You'll be getting off the morning train, and loving husband that I am, I'll be here so you can rush into my arms and tell me how much you've missed me. I've made friends with several of the guards. They frequent my shop to buy stationary to write home to their families. But I've mentioned several times that you'd be coming home soon on the train."

"And are you excited about that?" I asked,

wanting to know the finer nuances of our relationship.

"It'll be somewhat of an inconvenience to have my wife underfoot after a year apart. The guards sympathize. But I'm sure I'll adjust to your presence."

"I'm sure you will," I said wryly. "What of the locals? They've accepted you?"

"There's been a surge of Vichyssoise moving to the outskirts of the country to avoid the bombings and the derision of the rest of France. So yes, for the most part we are accepted."

Vichy, France had declared itself as an ally of the Nazi party. That part of France was still unoccupied by the Nazis, but there were rumblings Germany wasn't going to let it remain too much longer. The Nazi party didn't have allies. But for now, it would work to our advantage, though the thought of aligning myself with the enemy—even in pretend—didn't sit well in my stomach.

"So Peter and Helen are Nazi sympathizers?" I asked.

"That's the rumor," he said. "Though it hasn't been confirmed. I've been known to pass some critical information for Germany through my shop. Of course, that can be said for both sides of the war. It's quite a convenient establishment."

It was still dark, but there was a pearly sheen

of morning that hovered in the air so our surroundings began to come into focus. Everything was grey—as if every part of the country the Nazi's infiltrated was suddenly devoid of all color and life.

I kept my hand on Pierre's shoulder as we made our way through a thickly treed area. He squeezed my hand and I released him, hunkering low in the foliage. Hitler had definitely put his imprint on the station. The swastika flags flew like a beacon against a gloomy backdrop, and the emblems had been added to trains and the sides of the bricked station. I could see the barbed-fence, completed on the opposite side of the tracks to keep intruders out, but there was nothing on the side where Pierre and I were currently located.

Guards paced at strategic points, their machine guns at the ready, and there were shadows of people as they went into the station.

"There are less guards than usual," he whispered. "Too much celebration in town last night. This will work to our advantage."

"I'm assuming you're going to tell me what "this" is?" I asked.

He nodded. "I'm going to leave you here. I've got a car stashed and travel clothes waiting for me. I'll arrive like everyone else through the front door of the station. The first train of the day is always the fullest, so it'll help cause the most confusion. As soon as the whistle blows to alert the train arrival people will start rushing out on the platforms to meet the train. It'll be chaos, and the guards will fade to the far corner with their backs against the fence and watch who's coming and going. I've been watching them each day. It's a weak position, but they're not exactly the best the Third Reich has to offer.

"As soon as you hear the whistle start moving toward the outward platform," he said, pointing to the area. "It's a complete blind spot from where the guards will be standing and you can climb onto the platform easily from there. I've even placed and old crate for your convenience. Stay to the shadows as long as you can."

"And once I'm on the platform?" I asked.

"It needs to look like you've arrived on the train. Take this suitcase with you so as not to draw attention. And put your papers inside your coat pocket," he said, handing me a folded piece of parchment that looked well worn.

The station was starting to waken and cars crowded the main boulevard that led into the depot.

"I have to go," he said, and started to move away. And then he turned back and pulled me into his arms and gave me a kiss that had me seeing stars. His lips left mine almost as soon as it began, and he said, "Make sure you greet me like a woman who's been away from her husband for a year."

My lips felt numb and my legs were unsteady, but my voice didn't tremble. I was surprised. "If that's what the poor woman has to come home to, she probably found a Swiss lover to occupy her time."

He laughed. "Everyone knows the Swiss are terrible lovers." And then he held up my wrist. I hadn't realized he'd still been holding onto me. "Your pulse is pounding."

"It's rage," I said.

His grin was wicked. "Liar." And then he left me alone in the forest with nothing but blistered feet, a suitcase, and a lot of confusion.

ADA MAE

"Wait a minute," Ada said, thoroughly incensed. "That man kissed you? And you didn't punch him in the face? Tyler Brogan tried to kiss me on the playground once and I gave him a bloody nose. Nobody gonna touch me unless I wanna be touched."

Scarlet chuckled. "That's a good policy to have. But this was a little different circumstance. He was reminding me about the importance of the job at hand. If I hadn't acted like a wife in every sense of the word who was seeing her husband for the first time in a long while, then we both would have been put to death."

Ada scrunched up her face in thought. "So sometimes kissing a boy is better than death?"

Scarlet laughed again. "Most definitely. You'll find out when you're older."

"Mama is always saying that," Ada said with a sigh. "I'm ready to be older now."

"It'll be here faster than you know it."

Ada pouted. "She's always saying that too. How come you pretended to be those bad vishy people instead of regular people like last time."

"Vichy," Scarlet corrected. "Because sometimes you've got to dig in the dirt to get all the weeds out. Does that make sense?"

"I think so," she said. "Granny says it takes a thief to catch a thief."

"That's true too," Scarlet said. "You've got to be a good actor to be a good spy."

"So lying," Ada said, pressing her lips together.

"Yes, but lying for a good cause."

"Sometimes I lie when I tell granny I like her paintings," Ada confessed. "They're really bad."

"Sometimes being kind is more important than telling the truth," Scarlet said. "But it sounds like you'd make an excellent spy."

"Mama is like a spy with her investigations. Does that mean she's a good liar?"

Scarlet ran her tongue around her teeth and then pursed her lips, trying to decide the best course of action. "Your mama knows when it's appropriate to lie for the business."

"Well, she sure lied about Santa Claus, but I guess she was trying to be kind."

Scarlet's brows raised and she blew out a breath. "I might be old, but I don't remember children having these kinds of conversations."

"Daddy says it's because I'm a forty-year-old stuck in a six-year-old's body."

"Don't worry about Santa Claus and lies," Scarlet said. "Your parents just want to do the best they can for you. You're very lucky. And they'd never lie to you about important stuff."

Ada sighed and then yawned. "I know that. But I'm keeping the information in case I need to use it later."

"Just like a spy," Scarlet said. "Now do you want to go to bed or do you want me to finish my story?"

"I'm not sleepy," she said, stifling another yawn.

"Right," Scarlet said. "Where was I?"

THE SUITCASE

I watched the boulevard and the parking lot of the station closely for almost twenty minutes, but I didn't see anyone resembling Pierre.

My first thought was that he set me up. That he'd addled my mind with a kiss to deflect his real intentions and that I'd be walking straight into Nazi arms—just like Henry Graham. History really did repeat itself.

My second thought was that Pierre had been caught on the way to where he'd hidden his car. And if he'd been caught, there would be no one to greet me at the train, which would again draw attention since I'd be a lone woman on the platform.

Which left me with a third choice, which was to stay hidden in the trees until I could either reconnect with Pierre or send word to my SOE contact in London. To my way of thinking, none of the scenarios were ideal.

Of course, there was always a fourth choice. There was a chance that Pierre had been telling the truth and that the mission was legitimate. But like he'd said, I didn't need to worry about *who* to trust, but *how*.

The reminder made my decision for me.

I ran my hands over my hair to make sure I hadn't picked up any more greenery and then put on my hat. And then I painfully forced my feet into the shoes I'd been avoiding up to now. I closed my eyes briefly and breathed in through my nose. I'd experienced worse pain, but it didn't feel like it at the moment.

I reached down and picked up the suitcase Pierre had left behind. I'd been expecting for it to be empty, but there was considerable heft to it. I set it down immediately, deciding to open it quickly and see if there was any condemning evidence inside, but the whistle blew, announcing the arrival of the morning train.

It was as if someone had kicked an ant bed. People swarmed onto the platform from the station, and when it became too crowded, many moved to the platform on the other side so the train would be surrounded. Excited chatter rose as the train drew closer.

I picked up the suitcase again and started forward, keeping to the cover of the trees as I moved. My eyes were on the guards and I watched as they moved to the opposite side of the platform near the fence so they could see who was coming off the train, and I realized Pierre had been right. There was a blind spot exactly where he'd moved the crate so I could climb onto the platform.

I guess I'd found the *how* to my trust issue. And right now, I had to trust that Pierre would be on that platform to get me. Only I had to get there first.

I hefted the suitcase and moved as fast as I could. Adrenaline surged through me, and any pain I'd felt was gone, but I'd come to the end of the protection the forest provided. I could hide no more. I paused briefly just before I stepped foot into the open, and realized Pierre had chosen my herringbone travel suit with care. It blended into the drab grey of the morning.

Someone would have to be looking straight at me to see me, and that thought gave me the confidence I needed to move the rest of the way to the platform closest to me. The train was coming into the station, and everyone's attention was diverted in the other direction, including the guards. I reached the platform just as the train rumbled to a stop, and I hoisted myself and the suitcase onto the platform with little effort.

I kept to the edge, winding my way through people, until I was close enough to touch the black passenger car. The porters began opening the doors and people came flooding out with trunks and bags. They all had tunnel vision as they looked for their loved ones, so no one noticed me. And then I saw my chance, and I slipped behind a man who was occupied with folding his newspaper and climbed onto the step and onto the train. A man in a dark coat had his back to me, arguing with his wife about the weight of his luggage, and he bumped into me.

He turned quickly and said in German, "Pardon me," he said. "Please." He ushered me in front of him. "Go ahead."

"Thank you," I said, giving him a brilliant smile and using the handrail to steady my steps back off the train and onto the opposite platform from where I'd started.

I moved with the crowd to keep from getting run over, looking for a familiar face. There was a mixture of languages—French, German, Polish, Czech—and my suitcase kept knocking against the side of my knee as people jostled it passing by.

The guards were weaving back to their positions now that most everyone was off the train, and watery sunlight broke through the dreary skies even as the snow fell a little harder. I used my hand to block the sun from my eyes, hoping Pierre—no, Peter—would come into view. But he was nowhere to be seen. The spit in my mouth dried up and I could feel the pulse in my throat pounding wildly. I was a sitting duck.

And then I heard someone calling my name. "Helen!" and I saw Pierre step from behind a family who'd been clustered together in a tight embrace.

My relief and smile were genuine, and I cried out, "Peter!" I put my hand on my hat to keep it from falling off and rushed toward him. Gone was the spy I'd met in the woods, and in his place was the most dashingly handsome man I'd ever seen. His suit was fine and tailored, and he wore a long black coat and fedora.

He met me halfway and caught me in an embrace, and then he kissed me like he had before, lingering a little longer this time.

"So beautiful," he said, touching the side of my face with his palm.

I nuzzled against him, and then he leaned down and whispered something much too intimate in my ear. But I laughed gaily and gave him a taste of his own medicine, leaning in to give him a kiss that made the one he'd given me in the woods seem brotherly.

"All right," he said, smiling indulgently and tucking my arm in the crook of his elbow. "Now that you've gotten the attention of every guard in the station, maybe we should be on our way."

He took my suitcase and led me across the platform toward the station. It was almost odd to see something so normal. Travel was not so free and unencumbered outside of Germany. Trains were closely monitored by the Gestapo and checkpoints were scattered throughout Europe so people could present their papers.

"I'm just excited to see you darling," I said, batting my eyelashes.

There were shouts and the crowd surged backward, and I saw one of the guards raise his machine gun and bring the butt of it down on someone. Pierre stepped in front of me and had his arm across me protectively, but he was focused on the scene ahead. And then I heard the instructions in German.

"Inspection," one of the guards yelled.

I didn't know what had caused the sudden controversy, but someone had obviously gotten caught with something they shouldn't have. I looked down at the small suitcase Pierre held in his hand and wondered again if there was anything inside that would be a death sentence.

We were ushered into two lines, and Pierre squeezed my hand. I wasn't sure if it was out of warning or encouragement, but I stayed silent. Even with our considerable skills, there wasn't much either of us could do in a situation like this other than to let it play out.

The line moved quickly. The guards weren't concerned with people's belongings. It only took moments to open cases and trunks and riffle inside, or in several cases, dumping the contents out completely.

"Papers," one of the guards commanded when we got to the front of the line.

I handed my forged papers to Pierre and he handed both of our documents to the guard, and then the guard tapped his swagger stick on the top of the table and Pierre set the suitcase on it.

"Herr Beauchamp," another soldier said, coming up behind the one about to open our suitcase.

"Captain Rolfe," Pierre said with a curt nod.

I didn't think of my home in Whiskey Bayou often, but I did think of America and the freedoms I'd never given much thought to in my short lifetime. I missed the opportunities to speak freely and the friendliness of my fellow man. Since my arrival in Europe, everything I said was measured. Everyone I knew looked at each other with suspicion. And no one really knew what anyone was thinking.

The Germans had a formalness that grated against my rebellious nature, but self-preservation kept me in check. Which had probably been the reason my father had sent me away in the first place.

"You have claimed your wife?" Rolfe asked, his face stern as he looked me over. His lips were thin, but I'd seen interest in enough men's eyes to know when it was there.

"I have," Pierre said. "This is my wife, Helen."

I nodded and gave him a sly smile, keeping eye contact as I did so. I'd discovered keeping eye contact usually disconcerted men enough to get them off track. I couldn't have scripted better what happened next. The guard next to Captain Rolfe opened the suitcase and out spilled scandalous lingerie that I'd never seen before in my life. Both men looked at me and then back down at the lingerie. And then back at me again.

I smiled, my gaze never leaving Captain Rolfe. There was no point in flirting with the underlings. The rank had the power. And I'd learned to never waste an opportunity to put myself in the path of power.

"As you can see, gentlemen," Pierre said. "We're in a hurry to be home."

MARRIAGE

I was delighted to see the beauty of the city.

In the time I'd spent in Europe, destruction had been the commonality between different countries and the cities within them. War touched everyone, but Waldenburg sat like a postcard nestled between the mountains.

"Ksiaz Castle," Pierre said, driving comfortably up the winding roads into the town center. "Built in the thirteenth century."

"It's beautiful," I said. "Why'd you put lingerie in the suitcase? Did you know they would open it?"

"It was a hunch," he said. "Your file said men, including the enemy, were enamored by you. Therefore, I assumed you were a very attractive woman. And the soldiers here under Captain Rolfe have turned this into a city of decadence and debauchery. The drinks flow freely in the tavern, and many soldiers have been distracted by the women who work there. Sex has toppled more than one dynasty, and there's no point in not using our natural assets."

"Mmm," I said, trying to absorb the lay of the city. He'd been right about the trains. I could see several sets of tracks climbing into the mountains or veering into the trees. "Before I seduce the entire German army, are you going to tell me why I parachuted explosive components into Waldenburg."

"In due time," he said. "Enjoy the scenery. We won't be here much longer."

That was surprising news to me. I hadn't been told the duration of the mission before I'd left London, but I'd expected to be here for at least a few weeks.

It was a Gothic city with tall spires and brightly colored orange tile roofs, and the streets were paved with stones. It was a city that bustled with commerce and the lives of people who were doing their best to look the other way at what the Nazis were doing for their own self-preservation. Tram cars ran down the main streets as people got on and off for work or school.

"City market," Pierre said. "It's within walking distance from our apartment. You can get everything from pigs to rhubarbs, depending on the season and the farmer."

"Interesting combination," I said.

"Wait until you see how helpful the pigs have been," he said cryptically. "City Hall is there." He pointed to a more modern structure, but with the same Gothic architecture. "It's been taken over as a command center. This is Captain Rolfe's domain. He's taken over the Burgermeister's home attached to the side. Rolfe is an excellent politician. He wines and dines the elite and throws lavish dinner parties celebrating their success at liberating the city from those who are not of pure race."

"He succeeded?" I asked. "Completely?"

"Rolfe is a machine. Very calculating. Very thorough. This is a German province, but because of the proximity to the border there were a mixture of nationalities and races. The Jews went first. Then those of Slavic and Romani descent. More than a dozen twins were taken and all of the patients in the mental ward at the hospital were evacuated and put on the trains."

"Which means everyone who's left is pretending they don't know what's happening to their neighbors," I said. "Despicable."

"Agreed," he said. "Which is why I'm not in the least bit sorry that we're going to ruin people's lives while we're here."

"That's the most romantic thing you've said since we met," I said, my mouth quirking in a smile. "How's that? Did that sound wifely?"

"No," he said. "I'm not sure marriage suits you."

"I've often thought the same," I said, thinking that maybe Pierre Lavigne was more observant of human nature than I'd given him credit for. "It seems a stifling institution."

"I'd think that would depend on whether or not a couple can stand to be in the same room with each other."

"Are you married then?" I asked.

"I can't say," he said, his tone perplexed.

It seemed an odd answer. "It's a secret?"

"No," he said. "I can't say because I don't know the answer. I was married just before the war started, but my skills were more necessary to my country than to my marriage. I received a petition for divorce almost two years ago, but I've been too busy to see about it. I'd assume the magistrate would go ahead and grant her request after this long."

I arched a brow. "It seems like something you should check into next time you're in France."

"Why?" he asked, flicking his fingers off the steering wheel. "I never plan to marry again, so it's inconsequential."

"It must have been a memorable experience for you to be so blasé about it."

"It was impulsive and romantic. Which is what the young and stupid are known for. I truly never think on it, and I can't recall what she looks like. It seemed a good idea at the time, though I can't remember why we thought that. It's best not to get attached to anyone in this business."

"You plan to continue in the business after the war is over?" I asked, curiously.

"The business of secrets and lies never stops, even after the last bullet is fired. Someone has to do it."

I'd had the same thoughts.

There was a roundabout across from city hall and Pierre circled around until he came to the exit for a wide street that was busier than all the others combined. Rows of shops and bakeries and florists flanked both sides of the wide boulevard—which had recently been renamed *A.H. Strasse* after the Nazi leader.

"The stationary shop," Pierre said, gesturing to the left.

The storefront was large and painted black, and the windows were polished to a gleam. It sat between a bookstore on one side and an olive-green building with an ornate front door. There was a swastika insignia as plain as day on the door.

"You're kidding," I said. "The shop is next door to the Gestapo?"

"What better place to be," he said. "Hiding in plain sight. The best part is that our apartments are on the floors above it, and the walls are thin. So make sure you're vocal in your pleasure when we pretend to make love. I have a reputation to uphold."

THE PLAN

Pierre's comment reminded me how important it was to always stay in character. Our level of intimacy could mean life or death.

"If the walls are thin," I said, "how will you tell me what the plan is?"

"Have you ever heard the saying about the best way to eat an elephant?" he asked.

"Of course," I said. "A bite at a time."

He nodded. "And that's what we're doing to the army. This will be a coordinated attack. We have spies, as you know, in Paris. Most of the army supplies are manufactured there. Everything from uniforms and socks, to parachutes and weapons. The trains in Paris will be loaded in the morning with everything the army needs to survive the winter. There are supply trains heading to all of Europe. The train manifest says the shipment for this area will arrive Friday morning. Our mission, and the mission of the other teams scattered across Europe, is to make sure the Nazi army has a very uncomfortable winter. It gets cold in these mountains come January.

"It seems simple enough," I said. "What's the catch?"

"The catch is that we have to intercept the train, get on board, plant the explosives, and then jump off again before we're blown to hell and back."

"That seems like a pretty significant catch," I said.

"I didn't say it was easy."

"Do we have a team?" I asked, remembering the group I'd become close to in Marseille.

"The SOE has others in this area that have been in place for a while," he said. "And you were not the only person dropped into enemy territory. One person can't transport all of the detonation devices. Most explosive material is common and easy enough to explain if caught with it, but best not to have all the components together."

Behind *A.H. Strasse* was a narrow alleyway where shop owners, most of whom lived above their businesses, could enter privately. The Gestapo guarded the alley and gestured us through when they recognized Pierre.

"I've taken the liberty of soundproofing our

closet," he said. "If we need privacy I'll use the phrase, "She ordered lilac perfumed stationary.""

"And what if I need privacy?" I asked.

"You can use the phrase, "Six dozen wedding invitations.""

"Of course," I said. "That seems like something that would come up in everyday conversation."

"It is for stationary shop owners," he said. He pulled into the short drive behind a four-story narrow stucco building painted dark gold. There were no windows along the back—the expense had been reserved for the side facing the street.

"I hope there's not a fire," I said. "I don't like our chances of escape."

"There is a closet on the second floor where I've removed the paneling and loosened the mortar in the bricks. All we'd have to do it push and we could jump from the second floor."

"Let's hope there are no fires then," I said. "I've never been keen on jumping out of buildings onto a pile of bricks."

He laughed. "Jumping out of planes is much easier?"

"Always," I said. "If the chute doesn't pull you're assured immediate death. Jumping from buildings leaves too many variables as far as how much damage the body can sustain without actually killing you. Give me a quick death any day."

"That is something we can most definitely agree on," he said. "How are your acting skills?"

"They've served me well so far," I said, arching a brow. "Why?"

"Because we're about to come home after almost a year apart. If it doesn't sound like we're doing what normal couples would do in that instant, they're going to be suspicious. I just need to know if you have inhibitions."

I laughed, finding the statement funnier than he probably meant it to be. "Don't worry," I told him. "I can be completely convincing. Women have been making men think they're enjoying themselves since the beginning of time. I'm not sure a man has ever noticed when she's not."

He looked at me in surprise. "It sounds like maybe you've not known the right men."

I couldn't help myself and rolled my eyes. "You think? How long are we going to sit in the car? What are your acting skills like? Am I going to have to carry this thing or are you going to participate?"

This time, it was him who rolled his eyes, and he got out of the car and came around to open my door for me. There were two guards standing in the doorway of the building next to us, and a Nazi flag hung over the threshold.

They were facing each other in conversation, but I could tell their attention was on us.

Pierre took my hand and pulled me from the car, and then he swooped me up into his arms and ran into the house, both of us laughing like we hadn't a care in the world.

ADA MAE

"Whoa, whoa, whoa," Ada said, holding up her hands. "Are we about to get to the gross parts?"

"What gross parts?" Scarlet asked. "There are no gross parts."

"Uh, huh. Just like when we're watching your soap opera and they start ripping each other's clothes off, and then you send me to the kitchen to get us snacks so you can watch it by yourself. Why do they rip clothes like that? I'd be real mad if some man ripped my favorite shirt. I'd make him buy me a bunch more."

Scarlet chuckled. "It just happens some-times. In the heat of the moment. But it wasn't just some man. And it wasn't even real. Pierre and I had to pretend we were married, and that's what married people do."

Ada rolled her eyes. "Tell me about it. Now

I've got a little brother. Mom and dad are always doing gross stuff."

"That's good. It means they love each other. And sometimes when parents love each other you get a baby brother in the deal."

"I know all about sex," Ada said. "I read a book with pictures and everything."

"Hmm," Scarlet said. "I'm sure you did. But maybe you should ask your mom, just to make sure the book you read was telling the truth."

"I thought books always told the truth," she said, confused.

"Oh, no," Scarlet said, shaking her head. "That's why we've got a brain. We read and learn and go to school, and then we can use our best judgment. Because sometimes when something sounds like hogwash, that's because it is."

"What's hogwash?"

"It means it's a bunch of bull."

"Gotcha," Ada said. "What books did you read that were bull?"

"Hitler wrote a book. And I can tell you, that was a *whole* lot of bull."

Ada's lips pinched tightly and she said, "I imagine so."

"And the Nazi's used to publish pamphlets all the time. It was just propaganda to scare people into doing what they were told. That's why I never believe anyone plastered on the news screens or trying too hard to be in charge. I've been there, done that."

"What happened after you and Pierre pretended to do the gross stuff?"

"That's where things get interesting," Scarlet said. "Because if you remember, we only had a few days to get explosives made before the train came in. And we were living right next door to Gestapo headquarters."

"Hiding in plain sight," Ada said.

BACON GREASE

Three days in Waldenburg hadn't given me clarity to the mission.

Pierre and I had done an award-winning performance of married life, having broken a lamp and a bowl filled with fruit in the process of "reconnecting," garnering cheers and rowdy calls from the soldiers next door.

The detonators I'd smuggled into Germany were sitting under a plank in the floor, along with other familiar components that I guessed Pierre had picked up from other SOE agents or put together himself. It was up to us to put the explosives together, by combining common ingredients to make the nitroglycerine needed for dynamite. It was an unstable and dangerous process, and we were careful to keep everything separated. But I knew this would make our job more difficult because we'd have to assemble the components at the place of detonation, and we'd have to do it quickly.

I'd made myself at home in the lavish apartment, finding the kitchen well stocked and the bookshelves filled with an interesting assortment of literature, ranging from *Mein Kampf* to a book of bawdy poetry.

I spent my days listening through the wall about planned raids and names of families who were suspected of being Jewish supporters. I didn't write anything down, but I wouldn't forget. I was also able to hear Pierre open the stationary shop below and his conversations with customers. There was quite a bit of Nazi traffic through his doors, and hearing his answered, *Heil, Hitlers* and sympathetic conversation caused a brief hitch in my gut.

On my mission in Marseille, Henry Graham had been having those same kinds of conversations. He'd betrayed everyone—his country and me—and I couldn't help but wonder if Pierre was the same wolf in sheep's clothing.

When I wasn't eavesdropping on the Nazis next door, I spent the rest of the empty hours shopping in the market or having coffee and pastries with the book shop owner next door. Anna was rigid and proudly German, and she had no sympathy for the innocent who'd been ousted from their homes and taken away to concentration camps, but I needed to make friends with the locals like Pierre had done for the past year. I'd learned quickly that everyone loved Pierre, and I needed to fit into the cover he'd built.

We went about our regular lives in the day, but at night, we were out to be seen. I didn't have a true grasp of what Pierre's status was, but it seemed a mix of money and political, and the clout he had made me realize that he'd been building more than just a cover during his time here.

And at night, we'd come together in the soundproof closet and speak of who we'd met or any pieces of information that had been learned during the day. But the night he came upstairs with two pounds of bacon grease in glass jars was one I wouldn't forget.

"Do I want to know what you plan to do with all that bacon grease?" I asked once we were in the closet.

He arched a brow and his grin was a little wicked. "I definitely have plans for it. And you're involved."

"That's what I was afraid of," I said. "I've had some experience with bacon grease."

"That's what I've heard," he said. "It's how I knew you'd be the perfect partner. I needed someone whose every move would be in sync with mine."

"I guess most women would be flattered by

that," I said. "But I know I'm the one who's about to be left holding the…"

"Careful," Pierre warned.

"Explosives," I finished. "What did you think I was going to say?"

"I've learned over the last few days that I have no idea what's going to come out of that smart mouth."

I smiled. "Well, then. Mission accomplished."

He rolled his eyes. "Can you do it?"

"Build explosives powerful enough to destroy an entire train of supplies?"

"Yes," he answered.

"Of course I can," I said. "We'll have to carry the liquid components separately so they don't mix, but the bacon grease is a good substitute to make nitroglycerin. I read in one of the reports that there's a campaign in America for housewives to save their bacon grease to donate to the army."

"Yes, this wasn't easy to come by," he said. "Bacon grease is in high demand."

"I'm sure," I said, eyeing the two jars. "So the plan isn't as easy as jumping on a slow-moving train, planting explosives, and then jumping back off again. It's jumping onto a train without jostling volatile ingredients, and then building explosives once we're on board and running a detonation line long enough to destroy all the train cars carrying supplies, and then—assuming we don't blow ourselves up making the bombs—lighting the fuse and jumping off the train with enough clearance to avoid any shrapnel."

"Don't forget that the train will have armed guards."

"Right," I said. "Thank you for reminding me."

"Then, yes," he said. "That about sums it up."

"Piece of cake."

THE SIRENS

I met Jakob Novak by accident.

Pierre was quite the playboy and liked by the locals, and there was almost a sense of willful ignorance in the people who occupied the area —they drank and ate and laughed as if their fellow man weren't suffering just miles down the road at the nearest camp. It was unsettling and left a bitter taste in my mouth, but our role was different here.

We were one of them. And more importantly, the rumors had been spread that the wealth that lined Pierre's pockets was funding Hitler's vision. At least, that was the rumor.

I jumped into the fray of nights on the town with dinner and dancing into the late hours. There were no curfews like we'd had in Marseille. And they weren't strict on rationing. Captain Rolfe enjoyed his comforts, and he found that by letting everyone else remain comfortable then he got everything he wanted as well.

I found Pierre fascinating. He didn't treat me like other men did. He didn't fawn over me or stare lustfully. But it was easy to see his mind was brilliant and he was always playing a part. I wasn't sure if the man—the SOE agent—I spent time arguing with about everything from politics to American baseball was real or an actor. He was an enigma. And the more he confused me, the less I trusted him, because I couldn't figure him out.

But boy, did he play the part well. I fit easily into his arms when we danced, and our conversations flowed as if we'd known each other our whole lives. It was easy to lean into his kisses and affection so people could see how in love we were.

The soldiers frequented a tavern called the Der Rote Esel—The Red Donkey—and it was loud and rowdy, the drinks plentiful and the music and dancing the kind forbidden by Hitler. And though Captain Rolfe was what Pierre called a "good soldier," there was a streak of rebellion in him that was in opposition to his leader's vision. Pierre said Rolfe saw himself moving up the ranks and had aspirations of becoming greater than Hitler. A man like that was dangerous because he had no loyalty and he was a government unto himself, though the reports he sent back to Berlin were no doubt filled with their devotion and allegiance to their master.

It was a night where the Der Rote Esel was filled so that dancing couples spilled out onto the streets. The night was cold and snow fell in lazy flakes, but there was still a sheen of sweat on the bodies pressed close together.

I'd found a rhythm to Pierre's conversation as we danced through the room. He made deals and brokered trades between soldiers and locals alike, and he did it with the authority of a man who knew how to make life better for people or intrinsically worse. I wasn't sure if the people of Waldenburg were in awe of Pierre or afraid of him.

"You've been quiet tonight," he whispered, tucking my hair behind my ear. "Are you tired?"

"Never," I said. "I've missed this. Missed you. The Swiss are not so enjoyable in these things."

He chuckled and steered me smoothly through the crowd as the band played another song.

"You are more beautiful every time I look at your face," he said. "I'd almost forgotten what you looked like while you were gone, but now that I see you, I don't know how it's possible to forget such beauty."

The romance of his native tongue rolled over me. I couldn't speak, so I held him tighter. The crowd was raucous around us, but it was as if the noise had been canceled and all I could hear was him. There was the smell of sweat and beer in the air, but it faded next to the scent of his aftershave.

The sirens took us all by surprise, and the crowd rushed out the front door of the tavern until everyone stood in the streets looking up at the sky. In Marseille, when the sirens had gone off, it meant to find shelter. But the sirens we were hearing weren't our own, and the planes already buzzed overhead as they flew toward the Polish towns just across the border. It was their sirens that echoed off the mountains. And I watched in horror as the bombs fell from the planes and lit up the night sky like a heat light-ning storm over Whiskey Bayou.

Pierre and I stood at the back of the crowd, and I leaned against him as he wrapped his arms around me. People were dying, and the soldiers in the crowd cheered as if it were a cele-bration.

I didn't think much of the small man who came up and stood next to my right side. But he moved closer, until he bumped my arm, and then I looked over at him. He was thin and unassuming, and even looking straight at him I wasn't sure there was any distinguishing features about him that made him anything more than completely ordinary. He hadn't bothered with a hat and his face was clean shaven. He wasn't handsome or unattractive. He just…was.

"Jakob," Pierre said softly, the words a whisper in my hair.

"We need to meet," Jakob said. "The supply train is coming soon. There will only be one chance."

"This is too risky," Pierre said.

"I know, but I've been waiting for an opportunity for three days." Jakob's mouth barely moved with the words he spoke. "I can wait no longer."

"We'll meet you in the cellar in the bookshop," Pierre said.

Jakob nodded and disappeared as suddenly as he'd come. I held my questions, of which I had many, and I waited impatiently for several more minutes as the bombing continued. And then Pierre made sure to say his goodbyes to the tavern owner and a couple of soldiers, and then he put his arm around me and led me across the square toward the boulevard where our apartment was.

The streets were dark and deserted, but Pierre didn't stay to the shadows. We walked down the middle of the road. I could feel eyes on us, and I worried Pierre might be too cocky. I'd known the Gestapo in France. They were consumers of people and things. They cared about no one who wasn't the same as them. And they were cruel and violent. They would think nothing of shooting down someone like Pierre in the streets—someone of influence and who was well liked—if only to strike fear into the people they needed to strike fear into.

That moment hadn't come yet. For some reason, the Nazi party liked the attention and lavishness Pierre heaped on them. But it wouldn't last forever. And then someone would die. I'd seen it too often for it to not be true. I knew Pierre knew this as well as I did, but he was playing fast and loose anyway. I wasn't sure if he was a genius or an idiot.

He unlocked the door of the stationary shop and opened it so the little bell tinkled above us. The soldiers on duty would hear us come in next door, and they'd be listening as we made our way upstairs to our apartment, just as they always did. Sometimes they even joined our conversations through the walls.

Pierre moved into the stationary shop with familiarity, chatting about mundane things like what we needed to buy from the market the next morning. There was a private staircase in the back of the shop that led to our apartment, and I took off my wrap and pulled the pins from my hair, massaging my scalp as I followed Pierre. The blisters on my feet hadn't fully recovered, but we'd wrapped them good, and Pierre had somehow acquired soft Italian leather slippers so I could play my role without whimpering in pain with every step I took.

I wasn't sure what the plan was. I didn't know who Jakob was. And I didn't know what the safe room was in the bookshop. All I knew was that I had no choice but to follow Pierre's lead. And I was trying to keep my irritation at a minimum for being kept in the dark. Of course, I knew Pierre didn't trust me either, so that lessened the sting somewhat of him not sharing what seemed like important information.

I could tell by the devil in his grin that he was well aware of my aggravation, but he kept up a stream of conversation that moved from general information about some of our neighbors to asking if I was ready for bed, followed by a very explicit account of what he wanted to do to me once we got there.

I crossed my eyes at him and stuck out my tongue, and then I ran the rest of the way up the stairs, laughing seductively. He tugged my hand toward the bedroom and then put his finger to his lips as he closed the door loudly behind us. Then he ushered me into the large closet we shared.

I didn't know where the clothes in the closet I'd been wearing the last couple of days had come from, but they fit well, and Pierre had told

me they'd been hanging there since before the
Nazis had arrived. One of the first thing the
Gestapo had done when they'd taken over the
city was to search every apartment on the boule-
vard so they could eradicate those who didn't fit
Hitler's ideal.

But the clothing in the closet had been a
surprise, and it made me wonder how long ago
Pierre had chosen me for this mission.

I watched with curiosity as Pierre moved to
the middle of the back of the closet and reached
behind several dark suits, swiping his hands
along the wall and pressing in different locations
until there was a soft snick.

He gestured with his fingers to come
forward, and he held the suits back so I could
slide though a small opening in the wall.

"Reach your hand out," he whispered, his
lips pressed to my ear. "There's a stair rail.
Follow it all the way down."

I grasped the railing tightly and put one foot
in front of the other, searching for the steep
steps in total darkness. It was disorienting to not
be able to see shapes or the hint of what was
ahead of me or below. Then I felt Pierre on the
step above me and heard the secret door click
shut behind him. The space seemed to get
smaller the farther I went down, and I wondered
if Pierre would be able to get his broad shoulders through.

The air was hot and musky, and my breath was shallow as the walls closed in. I could no longer tell which direction was up or down, and panic started to claw at me as the darkness became consuming. I felt myself falling forward, and even as I had the thought that I'd be falling into an abyss of nothingness, my feet hit solid ground.

I stumbled and gasped as Pierre wrapped his arms around me.

"Steady," he whispered. "Are you all right?"

I nodded my head, but couldn't speak just yet. The world was starting to right itself, and I could see shadows forming in the darkness. There was light seeping in from somewhere in the room, and the air had grown cool and smelled like earth.

"We're safe here," Pierre said. "We're in the cellar of the book shop next door." I heard the familiar scrape of a match being lit, and he cupped his hand around the flame. "There's a door just there. Jakob is waiting."

I nodded and took a steadying breath and moved toward the door I could see clearly now. The iron knob was cool to the touch and I pushed it open, walking into a dank room lit only by lanterns. There was an old wooden table in the center of the room, and next to it stood Jakob, the man from the tavern. But he wasn't alone. In the corner stood an older, well-to-do couple who ran the book shop and lived in the neighboring apartment to ours.

"Scarlet Holmes," Pierre said. "This is Jakob Novak. He's an SOE agent out of Poland. Does excellent ground reconnaissance, and moves like a shadow."

"I heard of your work in Marseille," he said simply, nodding a hello.

"And you know Gregor and Anna," Pierre continued. "They're German citizens from Waldenburg, but volunteered their services to the SOE after the first raids were done in the city."

I almost wished I hadn't known that information. I'd been polite to our neighbors the few times I'd seen them, chatting with Anna about my time in Switzerland and my mother's death. But knowing they were German-born citizens who'd volunteered to become double agents didn't set my mind at ease. This was another element we had to take into consideration, because whether they were true to their word or not, I had no choice but to believe that they'd betray us at any moment.

ADA MAE

"Granny says to never trust anyone who chooses white wine over red," Ada said.

"Granny is the expert on such things," Scarlet said. "I probably should have asked Gregor and Anna which they preferred."

"I don't think I would've liked going down that dark hole. I get scared of the dark sometimes." She yawned and snuggled her baby doll closer.

"It's not my favorite thing either," Scarlet agreed. "I'm of the mind that I'd rather see what's trying to kill me than be surprised. It's why I never sleep in a car or airplane. I want to be awake if I'm going to die."

"That's very brave," Ada said. "I don't think I'd want to be awake."

Scarlet waved her hand dismissively. "It's not something you have to worry about for a long time, so there's nothing to be scared of in the dark. Though I have to confess, after my experience crawling down into that hole, I developed a bit of claustrophobia."

"What's that?" she asked.

"It means every time I get in a closed in space it feels like I'm in a coffin being buried underground."

Ada nodded. "You should get cremated. Then you won't have to worry about that."

"Already a step ahead of you. I'm going to have my ashes shot out of a cannon with a bunch of confetti and fireworks. It'll be a real party. And it'll be hilarious to settle on your Grandmother Dempsey's shoulders like dandruff. I'm going to haunt her for a long time."

"Daddy says you can't pick your parents," Ada said.

"That's true enough. I know that better than anyone." Scarlet stretched her legs, feeling the stiffness in her knees and wondered how long they'd been sitting there. "Are you getting tired? You probably need to go to bed. You know everyone is going to be up early."

"I'm not going to bed until I hear the end of the story," Ada said. "What did Jakob have to tell you that was so important?"

"Well, the information he gave us saved our lives," Scarlet said. "We didn't have all kinds of

technology back then like you do now. We had
to use our wits and sometimes make things work
out of necessity. We had street smarts."

Ada nodded. "Those were the good old
days…"

THE INVITATION

Pierre put his hand on the small of my back and guided me to the center of the room, and Jakob placed a roll of parchment about three feet in length onto the table. He swiped his hand across it and unrolled a well-used copy of a map, littered with markings and stains.

"The train arrives in just over fifty hours," Jakob said. "And from my understanding, you are working with volatile materials, yes?"

"Yes," Pierre confirmed.

"Then you cannot get onto the train before the Kreznow Pass," Jakob said. "That is the most logical place because it's a switch station, and there is a change of guards so there is a brief moment of time where there are no soldiers on the train. But you'd have to jump onto the outbound train to Austria, and then jump from the moving train onto the supply train at just the right moment."

"I see the problem," Pierre said, his mouth pursed in a thin line. "We need a more delicate approach so we don't blow up everything but the target. Hopping from train to train isn't the best way to keep our ingredients stable."

"What are our other options?" I asked.

"There is only one," Jakob said. "The supply train is coming from Paris, and like I said, will make a stop at the switching station just before the Kreznow Pass in the Alps. Travel through the pass is not difficult, but once the train clears the pass, there is a sharp curve in the tracks as it heads toward the Waldenburg station. But the speed of the train must be slowed considerably to make the turn safely.

"The tracks cut through the trees here," Jakob said, pointing to a spot on the map a few miles from the Kreznow Pass. "This gives you ample cover, and the train has to go slow enough that you should be able to step onto the last car as it passes by. You'll have to deal with the guards of course."

"Of course," Pierre said. "Does intelligence know how many soldiers will be on the train?"

"Two in the back, two in the middle, and two in the front," Jakob said. "But here is the tricky part."

"Oh, good," I said. "I was hoping you'd get to the tricky part."

Everyone stared at me for a few moments and Pierre said, "She's American," as if that explained everything. But the others seemed to accept that as excuse enough.

"Do you see this area here?" Jakob asked. "This is Schernburg Lake. A bridge was built for the tracks, and it's a twenty-meter drop to the water below. You've got to time the detonation so the train explodes over the water, but you must jump off the train before you reach this point." He pointed to another section of the map just before the lake. "There's a steep drop off into jagged rocks here, and jumping too late would mean death."

"I wouldn't expect anything else," Pierre said.

"Really?" I asked. "Because I'd prefer to expect survival."

"What fun is that?" he asked. "If you always expect to die, then you'll live your life to the fullest."

"That's very French of you," I said.

"Thank you," he said, nodding. "I think. Thank you, Jakob. I know you came here at great risk to tell us this information."

"Of course," he said. "I wish you both the best of luck. You'll need to plan your escape. There will be no coming back to Waldenburg."

"I'm sure we'll think of something," Pierre said, and then he nodded at Jakob and Gregor and Anna, and we left the way we'd come.

The sirens had stopped, and as we made our way back up the narrow stairs and back toward our apartment, I could hear the drunken singing of those wandering home from the tavern.

Pierre and I didn't say anything more about the mission that night. We were both deep in our own thoughts as we readied ourselves for bed and slid beneath the covers onto cool sheets. I'd found myself more than once snuggled up next to him in the night, with his arm tucked tightly around my waist, but I didn't mind. It had been a long time since I'd just been held, and it was nice. Besides, I didn't think Pierre even realized what he was doing.

But when we woke in the morning, we discovered a plan for our escape had literally been brought to our doorstep. The morning mail had been dropped in the door slot and lay in a pile on the floor. Among the envelopes was an invitation to one of Captain Rolfe's infamous parties.

Pierre reached down to pick it up and ran his finger under the seal. "Our presence is requested tomorrow night at nine o'clock for a formal gathering to recognize the arrival of his special guest, General Christoph Kuehler." Pierre stepped forward and pulled me into his arms, and I could feel his breath against my ear. "And if I recall, Captain Rolfe's borrowed abode has gardens that back up to Lisi Kamień Park."

My lips touched the pulse in his neck as I whispered, "That sounds like a convenient way to leave Waldenburg." My heart was pounding in my chest, and the time I was spending in such close proximity to an equally fascinating, yet aggravating, man was starting to get to me.

He took a step back, still holding up the invitation, and he said, "And look, this is stationary from my shop. Beautiful, isn't it?"

THE PARTY

I'd decided on a strapless formal gown in black that had intricate lacework across the bust and bodice. It was a little snug across my chest, but of all the selections in the closet it was the easiest one to move in and I'd always found black to be the best concealment for nighttime activities or blood. And I figured our future would hold the need for both.

"Lovely dress you're hardly wearing," Pierre said once I came out of the bedroom.

"Thank you, darling," I said. "If you play your cards right I'll let you find out what's under it later tonight."

He blew out a breath. "It can't be much."

"Exactly," I purred and moved past him toward the door. "Let's go. You know I hate to be late for a good party. And I've heard from everyone that Captain Rolfe's are the best."

Pierre helped me drape the fur wrap over my shoulders, and I pulled on my long black gloves.

"You look very dashing yourself," I said.

"If you play your cards right I'll let you find out what I'm wearing underneath later tonight."

I laughed out loud at his playfulness, and it wasn't an act. I wasn't used to men like Pierre—a man who didn't try to seduce me at every turn—a man who looked at my face instead of undressing me with his eyes. It was a breath of fresh air and an annoyance all at the same time. We'd been in each other's company for more than a week now, sleeping next to each other, pretending to be husband and wife. I'd be lying if part of me wondered if he found me attractive. Or maybe he wasn't interested in women at all.

When we stepped outside to our car there were more soldiers next door than usual, and all of them looked my direction. They'd heard Pierre's comment about the dress I was hardly wearing and obviously had come to see for themselves.

I gave them a smile as Pierre helped me into the car, and then he addressed a few of them by name before getting behind the wheel. The drive to Captain Rolfe's was short, as it was just at the end of the boulevard and across the square.

There was a procession of cars waiting their turn for guests to be let out at the front door. The house shone like a beacon in the darkness —every light on each floor turned on—and a huge flag with the Nazi regalia hung down the front of the house like a banner.

"Are you ready?" Pierre asked. "You've been very quiet."

"I'm ready," I said. "It's just sinking in that this is the end."

"Will you miss me, darling?" he asked, cheekily.

I fluttered my lashes and said, "Of course. How could I possibly go on without you?" But there was part of me that wondered if it was true. And by the expression on his face, I wondered if he knew exactly what I was feeling.

"How were you able to get our supplies hidden?" I asked, changing the subject. "Are you sure no one saw you."

"Oh, everyone saw me," he said. "But they didn't know what I was doing. There's an SOE agent who works as a nurse at the hospital, and she and I have been known to be seen together from time to time during your absence. I'm a cad, darling, you'll have to forgive me."

"Mmm," I said, looking out the window.

"But her home is conveniently located on the side street facing city hall and this house," he said. "And her back door leads out into the woods. So I'm sure anyone who saw my car parked in her driveway early yesterday thought nothing of it. And I was able to slip out the back and hide our supplies and the explosives."

"It's nice that you play so many steps ahead in this game of chess," I told him. "Your skill is rare."

"You have it as well."

"I know," I told him. "Which is why it's nice to work with someone else who can do it. Though it makes me feel as if I'm not pulling my weight."

"I've been in this cover a long time," he said. "Almost to the point where this identity has become easier than my old one. I've had time to plan my moves and orchestrate the cast of players and assess potential fallout from any given decision or situation. But you were the missing piece. This is a two-person job. I knew that even if I didn't like it. I prefer to work on my own."

I nodded, understanding. "Because then you have only yourself to count on."

"Exactly," he said. "But sometimes the job calls for something more. Your reputation preceded you. I'd heard rumors of you before I ever read your file. They said you were fearless and ruthless, and sometimes reckless. But that you were brilliant and loyal and determined. They said when it came down to the wire, that you could make the hard choices. And I knew because of the betrayal you'd experienced that you'd be more sensitive to those working around us.

"I've been here a year. I'm used to seeing the same faces day in and day out. But it's the same faces that can stick a knife in your back. I knew you'd bring the fresh perspective I needed. I saw how you looked at Gregor and Anna. I'd have been disappointed if you hadn't looked at them that way. Though I can assure you've they've more than proven themselves an ally to the SOE through great personal tragedy of their own."

"Why are you telling me this?" I asked curiously.

"I don't know," he said, shrugging. "But it seems fitting considering we could be dead before morning. I just wanted you to know that it has been a pleasure to work with you. And whatever happens on that train, I trust you'll do the job. But if something happens to me or I'm wounded…"

"You want me to leave you behind," I said knowingly. "And you'll do the same if something happens to me."

"Yes," he said. "This is not the business for personal attachments."

I smiled then. "I don't think I was put on this earth to have personal attachments with anyone. Some of us aren't so lucky."

"Or maybe we are the lucky ones."

I reached over and held my hand out, waiting until his fingers twined with mine. "Whatever the case," I said. "The pleasure has been mine. I'll buy the first round after the war is over."

"That's a deal," he said, just as he parked the car in front of the mansion.

Uniformed men opened each of our doors, and I held out my hand to be helped out of the car. It was glamour and glitz, and it reminded me of France before the invasion. The guests were here to be seen and photographed, and I wasn't sure Hollywood could have done a better job.

A party of this size and extravagance costs money, and it was something of a slap in the face to all the people who were sacrificing clothes and food because of the shortages. I didn't know where Captain Rolfe's funding came from, but he obviously wanted to impress General Kuehler. And from what I'd seen, a man who had funding and wanted to impress his superiors generally had his own political delusions of grandeur.

Pierre handed our invitation to the man at the door, and I shrugged out of my fur stole and handed it to the man checking coats. His gaze was glued to my dress and he dropped the fur twice before finally figuring out how to drape it on the hangar.

"I don't think he was prepared for you," Pierre whispered, putting his hand on my back.

I leaned into him and said, "Darling, men never are."

"You do look lovely," he said. "It's quite nice to have the most beautiful woman in the world on my arm. But also inconvenient. Because that means we'll be wildly popular tonight."

"Who are all these people?" I whispered as we moved to the top of the staircase that led into the ballroom. "I don't recognize anyone."

An orchestra played a waltz and the lights from the chandeliers glittered on the heads of the elite as they floated across the floor. The French doors had all been thrown open so a cool breeze swept into the overheated room, and lanterns lit the garden romantically.

"You might see a familiar face or two," Pierre said. "But there are dignitaries here from all over Germany. This is not a local gathering. Captain Rolfe has plans for his career that I think Hitler has not been made aware of. But he'll know after tonight."

"And how did we get invited to an event such as this?" I asked.

"Because we have someone on the inside who made sure we got an invitation," he said. "Rolfe won't think anything of it. I've been donating handsomely to his secret campaign fund, and filling his head with aspirations far beyond his grasp. But his ego is large, so it's not such a hard task."

A waiter passed with glasses of champagne on his tray and Pierre grabbed two, passing one to me. And then he held out his arm and I hooked my hand in the crook of his elbow as he led me down the wide curved staircase.

"I know many of these faces," he said in a low voice. "Everyone here is clawing for something—like a bushel of crabs waiting to pull down whoever is closest to the top. They're brutal and ruthless, and decadence and deviance are their vices. Hitler has lost control of this part of the country from within his own ranks. They'll stage a coup soon. But in the meantime, do not leave my side, not even to go to the powder room. The men here will not think twice about taking what isn't theirs. You'll start to see the façade of niceties fade as the drinks flow more freely and inhibitions are lost."

"Then it looks like we have some time to kill," I said. "What should we do?"

"I say we dance and look like two people who are very much in love," Pierre said. "Rolfe keeps looking in our direction. He's taken with you. But for tonight, we'll only have eyes for each other."

THE ESCAPE

There'd be no going back to the quaint apartment where Pierre and I had played at being
husband and wife. I knew that, so I clung even
harder to him as we swayed in time to the music.

"Are you ready?" he whispered in my ear,
touching the small of my back lightly.

"Always," I said, looking up at him seductively, a small curve on my lips.

He'd been right about the decadence and
deviance coming to light the longer the drinks
flowed. I'd watched countless couples disappear
to upstairs rooms, the gardens, or even the
curtained alcoves at the edge of the ballroom.

I hadn't left Pierre's side, just as he'd
instructed, and I appreciated his wisdom. More
than once a man had cut into our dancing and
tried to whisk me off the dance floor, only to be
stopped by Pierre. For anyone who saw us, we

looked like a devoted couple who couldn't wait to be alone together.

Captain Rolfe's party was exactly what we needed to make our escape.

Pierre leaned down to kiss me, fitting my body against his snugly. There were other couples on the dance floor, but I saw only him, and inch by inch we danced our way toward the open French doors.

"Peter," Captain Rolfe said, intercepting us before we could disappear. "I would like to introduce you to some friends of mine. I think you'll find them well connected and important to know."

"Of course," Pierre said smoothly. "Helen and I were just about to take a stroll through the gardens."

His finger rubbed hypnotically across my shoulder, and he leaned in to kiss my temple. Rolfe would have had to have been a fool not to realize what he was interrupting.

"I see," Rolfe said, arching a brow and then eyeing my décolletage with something sinister in his gaze. "I'm going to gather the others. I'll meet you in my office in half an hour. That should give you plenty of time to enjoy the..." his gaze swept over my body again and I resisted the urge to shudder. "Gardens," he finished.

"I'll meet you there," Pierre said, nodding

his head in thanks, and then leading me through the doors and onto the balcony.

There was only the shadow of a moon, and lanterns lit the gardens in a soft and secret glow. I heard rustles and giggles from the shrubbery, but Pierre took my hand and we hurried down cobbled paths like naughty children. He swept me into his arms and into a kiss in full view of the house. I'd felt Rolfe's eyes on us as we'd walked away, and I knew he was still watching.

"The gazebo," Pierre whispered, nipping at my lip.

I shivered. There was something exhilarating about being in Pierre's arms—danger and daring and romance—I was completely swept away.

He maneuvered us through the arched door of the gazebo. His eyes were hard and searching, looking for those lurking in corners or elicit couples we might stumble over in surprise, even as his touches were gentle. He was a contradictory man.

The music from the orchestra had faded. Complete darkness surrounded us, and he pulled me close. I wondered what he was doing. There was no one to see us, and our time was running out before Rolfe would expect him back at the house.

But then I somehow knew he was going to kiss me. His hands rested on my hips and his breath was soft across my lips. And then every thought in my head ceased as his mouth took mine. This wasn't like the kisses we'd shared before. It felt…real.

When he pulled away the blood was rushing in my ears and my heart was pounding in my chest. It was so dark I wouldn't have known he was there if I hadn't been holding on to him. He put his finger against my swollen lips so I didn't speak, and then he released me and moved away. My vision was adjusting to the darkness and I saw shadows where there had been none before.

"It's now or never," he said.

Then he took my hand and we disappeared through the hedges and into the heavily treed woods that surrounded Waldenburg. And then we started running.

The lace on my dress snagged branches and tore in places, and my feet rubbed at the same spots where my blisters had finally started to heal. But it didn't matter. The only thing that mattered was putting distance between us and them.

Almost a mile from Rolfe's estate, Pierre stopped and moved pine boughs and dirt to reveal the bags he'd left there the previous day. He opened one of the bags and tossed me a pair of dark men's trousers and a black jacket that would cover my pale skin.

I kicked off the black-strappy dress shoes I wore and barely had to tug at the strapless gown for it to fall to my waist. I pushed it down the rest of the way and stepped out of it. I knew Pierre was watching me.

"You weren't kidding when you said you weren't wearing anything beneath the dress," he said, his voice sounding choked.

I didn't normally disrobe in front of men I wasn't intimate with, but there was no use for modesty when time was of the essence.

"Why would I kid?" I asked. "I told you you'd get a chance to see what I wasn't wearing later tonight. If we live through this, maybe you'll get another chance."

"Oddly enough, I think I'll feel a lot safer on a train full of explosives than seeing you naked again. You're a dangerous woman, Scarlet Holmes."

"And you're driving me crazy," I hissed.

I dressed quickly and almost groaned as I put the black silk slippers on my feet. And then I watched unabashedly as Pierre stripped out of his white shirt, exposing a ridged chest and abdomen. He pulled on a black shirt that was boxy in style and unlike anything I'd seen while in Europe, and he left his black tuxedo pants on, exchanging boots for his dress shoes.

He shoved all of our clothes in the empty bag and then buried it back under the pine boughs. And then he reached for the other bag and strapped it to his back.

We'd packed the explosives carefully, enough for five charges in all, and we'd separated the liquids into their own containers so there was no chance of them accidentally mixing. But all it would take was a fall or for one of the containers to break, and this mission would be over before it started.

Kreznow Pass was less than ten miles from Waldenburg, but the path was treacherous. When Pierre didn't show for the meeting in Rolfe's office, they'd come searching for us and eventually figure out that we were no longer in the garden. The search would buy us some time but not much. Someone with keen eyes would be able to follow our trail, but they'd have to wait until daylight. And by that time, we'd be on the train.

We didn't speak for miles, not until the snow started falling as our elevation increased the closer we got to the pass.

"We can stop here for a moment," Pierre whispered. "How are your feet? Are you cold? You've barely any clothes on."

"I'm fine," I told him. "My heart is pounding so hard I'm not sure I'll ever be cold again. Why did you kiss me like that back in the garden?"

"Because I wanted to," he said simply.

"And what do you think about it?" I asked.

"I think I'd like to do it again," he said. "Maybe once we're back on allied soil and Nazis aren't on our trail. What do you think of it?"

"I think we should get moving," I said. "The sooner we get to allied soil, the sooner you can kiss me again."

I saw the flash of white teeth as he grinned. "Do you remember the map Jakob showed us?"

"Every detail," I said. "We can rest again once we get to the Kreznow Pass. Let's go."

He nodded and we traversed the miles quickly. I had to admire Pierre's form as he gracefully maneuvered uneven terrain without jostling the backpack. It was a volatile situation. Getting to the train in one piece was as dangerous as setting the explosives themselves.

"This is good," he said, coming to a stop. "The tracks are just there, and we'll be able to see the train coming from this angle as it comes through the pass. It'll still be dark, so that's to our advantage."

I knew he was trying to reassure me. There were so many things that could go wrong at any given moment. And we hadn't even gotten to the point where we had to get back *off* the train.

"You should try to rest for a bit," Pierre said. "If the train is on time we should have a couple of hours before we need to move into position."

He took a knife from his boot and cut several

boughs of pine, enough to make a soft place to lay. And then he cut a few more and waited until I sat down on the makeshift bed.

"It's not a down quilt, but it'll help with the cold," he said, laying the large boughs on top of me. "I'm going to find some water. I hear a stream not far off."

"You know this is madness, right?" I asked. "The timing of everything has to be perfect. There is no room for error."

"Are you scared of dying?" he asked.

"No, of course not," I said, waving away the concern. "I'm scared that the explosives won't detonate while the train is over the bridge so it falls into the lake. If we're going to die, I want to make sure we complete the mission."

"You're a hell of a woman, Scarlet Holmes."

I liked the way he said my real name.

"Yes, I know." And I snuggled under the pine boughs and fell asleep.

THE TRAIN

Pierre had been right. We were in the perfect location to see the light of the train coming from a good distance away.

We'd each gotten some rest and water, and I was moving and stretching, trying to get the blood flowing in my legs. The cold was making me lethargic, and I was afraid my muscles would cramp when it was time to get onto the train. I wasn't an expert on train jumping, by any means, but it seemed like it was important to have control of all faculties while making the attempt.

We'd already scouted the area. I remembered what Jakob Novak had told us about how important it was for the engine driver to slow to the proper speed before he all the way through the Kreznow Pass. We'd wait in the trees at the sharp bend in the tracks until the last train car was passing by, and then we'd make our move.

"What do you see?" I whispered.

Pierre looked through the binoculars and didn't answer me for a time, but then he said, "The train has armed guards, as we expected. I could see them as the train rounded the first bend after the pass. Are you ready?"

"I am," I said, nodding even though I knew he couldn't see me in the dark. He'd given me the backpack full of explosives so he could take care of incapacitating the guards without breaking anything in the bag. It was secure on my back, and the weight of responsibility felt like lead as the train came toward us.

We both stood hidden behind large pines as the rumble of wheels on the tracks grew louder. And then there was a squeal of brakes as the speed slowed to a crawl and the front of the train made the sharp turn right in front of us.

Patience was agony as we waited for every car to pass. And then finally, the caboose arrived.

Pierre hopped up onto the back rail with ease, taking the two guards completely by surprise. I heard the snap of a neck, and then he crushed the other's windpipe in mere seconds, and then he held out his hand to me and I stepped onto the back platform.

We both pushed the guards off the back of

the train and they fell with a soft thunk, and then Pierre lifted the latch on the back car door and we slipped inside. It was full of crates stacked floor to ceiling with only room to walk down a center aisle.

"This is it," Pierre said, pointing to the stamped label on the side of the crate that said *socken.* "You start here and I'm going to go on ahead and see if I can find the other guards."

I nodded, but I was already on my knees and carefully removing items from the backpack. Making bombs was a little like cooking—it was all about following the recipe and not getting impatient. My hands were steady as I capped off the first explosive and tucked it between two of the crates, and then I packed up my things and unfurled the detonation cord, trailing it behind me as I went into the next car, and then the one after that.

The train had sped up considerably after it had cleared the sharp curve, and I knew my time was running out before we got the bridge that passed over the lake. I'd just finished putting together the third explosive, and I was running the detonation cord into the next compartment when I came across two dead soldiers.

I hadn't seen Pierre since he'd left me to build the first device, but he'd obviously been successful in his hunt for the guards. Sweat dripped freely from by brow and into my eyes as

I worked on the fourth charge. We had to be getting closer to the bridge. The train was moving at a steady speed now, and the window of opportunity to jump was narrowing.

After the fourth device was finished, I moved quickly through the next cars, the detonation cord trailing behind me, but I heard the grunts and scuffles of fighting before I opened the next car door. I hesitated briefly, wondering what the situation was I'd be walking in on, and I took out the knife my father had given me before he'd sent me away.

I left the backpack on the floor of the car, and I attached the detonation cord roll to my belt loop so it trailed behind me. I knew there wasn't time to build the fifth device, but I still had to light the charge.

I didn't think as I unlatched the door. All I knew was that Pierre was in there, and despite what I'd told him, there was no way in hell I was leaving him behind. There were bright flashes of light as bodies twined together and fists flew and legs kicked. The smell of sweat and blood was heavy, and Pierre landed a punch that knocked one of the guard's heads back so hard he'd be seeing stars for a while.

"Get off the train," he said, panting. "We're almost at the bridge. Light the charge."

"I'm not leaving without you," I said.

"You promised."

"Shut up! I'm not leaving without you," I repeated.

Pierre got in a solid shot to the guard's midsection—enough to double him over—and I ran up behind him and kicked the back of his knee so he fell to the ground. It was all the advantage Pierre needed to bring his knee up under his chin and knock him out.

"There's no time for me to yell at you," he said, jerking open the side door of the car.

I sliced the detonator cord with my knife and then dug in my pocket for the matches. My hands weren't so steady now, but I managed to light the match and touch it to the end of the cord.

"Go," I said, and we ran toward the open door.

It was odd because it seemed like I heard the shot long before I felt the bullet go into my body. The other guard had gotten his wits about him long enough to pull the trigger. Pierre put his arm around, pulled me against him, and we launched into the air moments before the train went across the water.

We hit the ground hard, and Pierre tucked me into his body as we rolled across branches and pinecones and rocks. I couldn't breathe. The wind had been knocked out of me. And the pain in my hip felt like someone was pressing a hot poker into flesh and bone.

The Pierre was up on his knees, tearing part of his shirt and wrapping it tightly around me. He was saying something, but I couldn't hear. I could only see his lips moving.

Then the ground shook and the sky lit up. My hearing came back with a whoosh as each of the devices exploded like rapid fire, and chunks of fiery metal and bridge flew into the sky. It wouldn't be long before the fiery pieces were raining down on top of us.

"Got to move!" Pierre yelled. He hefted me onto his shoulder and started running toward the mountains and safe passage, even as the flaming shrapnel pierced the trees and lit fire to the forest around us.

ADA MAE

Scarlet thought she'd maybe gone too far when all Ada could do was stare back at her with her mouth hanging open.

"You'll catch flies with your mouth open like that," she said.

Ada snapped her mouth closed, but her eyes seemed to grow larger. "Did it hurt getting shot and blown up?"

Scarlet thought about it for a moment, not sure she had accurate words to describe what it had *really* felt like. "I'd certainly had better days during the resistance."

"I should think so," Ada said. "But it was quite romantic for Pierre to carry you into the mountains like that until you could be rescued. He must have been very strong."

"He certainly was," Scarlet agreed, her throat closing with emotion. She didn't often think of Pierre. Maybe because the memories were both treasured and painful.

"Do you still have the bullet hole in you?" Ada asked.

"I can do one better than that," Scarlet said. "I've still got the bullet in me. Right in my hip. The doctors said it was pressing just in the right place and if they removed it there was a chance I might not be able to walk like I should. And a spy that can't walk right is generally a dead spy. Though I did know a woman once who climbed across the Alps with a wooden leg."

"Wow," Ada said.

"Yep, I set off metal detectors everywhere I go. I've been real lucky. No lead poisoning or anything."

"How did they rescue you?"

"Pierre stole a car from a small village a few miles away, and we drove all the way to Austria. Then he put as many layers of clothes on both of us as he could, scooped me up in his arms, and he carried me into the mountains. It took us almost a full week to get to Switzerland. He could have gotten there much faster if he hadn't been carrying me, and I told him to leave me behind. But he never left me. I don't know how the Nazi's never caught up with us."

"He must have loved you a lot," Ada said. "I don't know if I'd ever carry anyone over the mountains."

"You'd do the best you could if you really loved them."

Ada looked down at the shiny gold medal. "Did Pierre get a medal like yours?"

"Not like mine," Scarlet said. "He was French, so his country awarded him a medal right after the war."

"I bet yours is bigger," Ada said.

"Take out the velvet casing under the medal."

Ada carefully removed the gold medal and laid it in her lap, and then she pulled at the blue velvet beneath it. She gasped and said, "You've got another medal in here. Why are you hiding it? How come you don't wear them? I'd pin them right to my dress every day. I bet Paris Wheeler doesn't have anything like this."

"I can assure you she doesn't," Scarlet said. "That's Pierre's medal. France gave it to me for Pierre."

"How come?"

"Because by the time they got around to giving the medals, Pierre had already died."

Ada's lips quivered and she said, "Oh, that's sad. I bet you were lonely without him."

"For a time," Scarlet agreed. "But the thing about life is that you've got to go on living it, and I had a lot of living to do."

"That sounds like something mama would say."

"That's because your mama is a Holmes, and she's a smart lady."

Ada pursed her lips and nodded like she'd heard that bit of information before. "I still want to know what happened in the mountains. How come when you got across to the other side the Nazis didn't arrest you?"

"Because Switzerland was neutral territory," she said. "And I don't remember much of what happened in the mountains. I remember the cold, and Pierre building a fire to keep us warm at night. But the days spent there were a blur. I remember him kissing me as we finally stepped foot in Switzerland, and then the next thing I knew I was waking up in a hospital bed and I was all alone."

Ada gasped. "He just left you?"

Scarlet laughed. "I'd thought so. But he was looking for a preacher. Crazy things happened during the war. It was a different time back then. And when he came to me in the hospital, dragging the preacher behind him, I couldn't think of anything more romantic than marrying him right then. He'd even used his connections back in London to check and make sure he was really divorced from his first wife.

"But you hardly knew him!" Ada said.

"I told you crazy things happened during the war. When every day is life and death, the decisions you make tend to be a bit more impulsive. But I didn't regret it one bit. We grew to love each other very much, and we had some grand adventures together."

Ada yawned again and rubbed her eyes.

"Speaking of grand adventures," Scarlet said. "I think it's time you went to bed. Santa has probably long since come and gone."

"Okay," Ada said, scooting off the chair. "But I wanna sleep in here with you. This is a good room, and I like the way the fire crackles."

"Has anyone ever told you no before?" Scarlet asked.

"Not very often," she said. "Daddy says I have charm."

"You've got something all right," Scarlet said. "Come on then, get into bed."

Ada climbed into the four-poster bed and snuggled under the heavy quilt. "Will you tell me more stories about your adventures with Uncle Pierre?"

"Another adventure for another day," Scarlet said. "Now tuck in."

Ada yawned again and her eyes drifted closed. "Good night, Aunt Scarlet," she slurred. "I'm real glad that you're mine."

Scarlet brushed the girl's hair back from her forehead and said, "I'm real glad you're mine too."

ORDER NOW!
FRONT LINE FRANCIS

It wouldn't be the South if there weren't proverbial skeletons in everyone's closets.

We certainly had our fair share in my family, and I knew other families had their fair share too, because we still talked about them in the checkout line at the Piggly Wiggly or with the cashier at Dairy Queen while waiting on an ice cream sundae.

It was January and dreary and cold in Whiskey Bayou, Georgia. I'd temporarily moved back home due to the fact that my boyfriend, Nick Dempsey, had proposed and I'd had a moment of panic where I saw myself the last time I'd been about to get married—big poofy white dress and cake for two hundred—only to catch my fiancé boffing my archenemy in our honeymoon limo.

They say lightning doesn't strike the same

place twice, but the proposal and subsequent panic attack were enough that I knew I needed some time and space to think about the proposal and being married to Nick for the rest of my life.

So I did what any girl does when unsure of the future. I moved back home with my mother. There are two problems with this. One: I worked in Savannah and the drive was a real bitch. And two: I was living at home with my mother.

Don't get me wrong. I love my mother dearly. And maybe we're more alike than I'm comfortable admitting. But living in the same house with her is enough to put me over the edge. Not to mention she's newly married and the walls are thin at Casa de Holmes.

Needless to say, I'd spent the last couple of weeks since the infamous proposal working as much as humanly possible so I wouldn't have to act like an adult and face my issues head-on. I had to admit, I was missing Nick. I'd gotten used to him. Which was really what marriage was all about—getting used to someone enough that you didn't want to murder them if you had to spend more than a few hours a day with them.

I was currently sprawled out on the leather couch in Kate's office, regretting the second cinnamon roll I'd just devoured and wondering how much Jillian Michaels butt clenching I'd have to do to make up the calories. My best friend, Kate McClean, owner of the McClean Detective Agency, sat in the chair just across from me.

That's when I heard the ruckus from down the hall. I was the daughter of a cop. And Kate was a former cop. So unless there was active gunfire neither of us were known to sweat the small stuff. Okay, maybe I sometimes sweated the small stuff, but it usually had to do with Black Friday specials and Louboutins being on sale. I was a seven, so my size always went fast.

"I'm here to see my niece and you can't stop me," a familiar voice—both fragile and four-star general—roared over me like a freight train. "I've got a .44 in here and I'm not afraid to use it. Better step out of my way, Elvira."

My eyes widened and I saw the pure fear on Kate's face at the thought of my Aunt Scarlet tangling with Lucy, the gatekeeper for the agency. Nobody made it past Lucy unless they were an employee or a client. I had my suspicions about Lucy. The two most prominent being that she'd worked for the CIA at some point or that she was a vampire—though I hadn't really figured out how she got around the whole sunlight issue.

We both shot up to a standing position and started running, but we went through the door at the same time and got stuck. It was then I noticed Lucy standing at the end of the hallway, her red lips pressed firmly together as she stood her ground. But Aunt Scarlet had worked as a spy for the OSS during World War II and she'd outlived five husbands, so nothing much intimidated her.

"Aunt Scarlet," I called out, shoving past Kate.

Aunt Scarlet was digging in her purse and pulling out a .44 revolver the size of a cannon. It was so heavy she couldn't lift it and she shot a hole in the floor between Lucy's feet.

I guess that was enough to stun Lucy because Scarlet pushed right by her and headed straight for us.

"I don't remember that gun having such a sensitive trigger," Scarlet said. "That sucker packs a punch. It was like getting kicked in the hot box by a mule."

I was afraid to ask what she meant by "hot box" but I'd gotten pretty good at interpreting Scarlet-speak over the course of my life. It had been three years since I'd last seen her, and the trauma of it all made it feel like yesterday. My mother was going to have kittens.

Scarlet was my father's aunt. Which meant she was my great-aunt. And she was our skeleton in the closet. She'd grown up as a Holmes in Whiskey Bayou during the Great Depression, and the family gossip was that she'd been shipped off to Paris by her father because she'd been having affairs with a couple of married men and they'd challenged each other to a duel, agreeing that the winner would get to keep Scarlet to himself.

Apparently Scarlet had been quite a looker in her day—a dead ringer for Ava Gardner, some people said—but she'd been rather loose with her virtue. Scarlet had never seemed to mind. When I was twelve, she'd told me it was better to be loose with your virtue than loose with your bank account. If I'd listened to Scarlet I'd probably be a lot more sexed up and a lot richer.

The days of Ava Gardner had long passed, and Scarlet now looked like Hannibal Lecter had put all of her bones in a skin bag and shaken them up so nothing quite fit together. She got around better than she should have for someone her age, and she attributed it to the fact that she'd smoked unfiltered cigarettes when she was younger and her insides were pickled from highballs.

The black wool coat she wore swallowed her whole and she'd left it unbuttoned, displaying a leopard-print velour jogging suit beneath. She wore white tennis shoes that were so bright they hurt to look at and a magenta scarf was wrapped around her neck. Her hair was a shock of white that had been permed within an inch of its life and shellacked with such success that not even the misty rain and frigid winter wind had budged it. She topped off the look with the signature bright red lipstick I'd never seen her without.

"I smell cinnamon rolls," she said, shoving her gun back in her handbag and brushing past me and Kate. "I didn't get breakfast."

Scarlet followed her nose into Kate's office and shrugged out of her coat, handing it to Kate to hang up. She left the scarf around her neck.

"Do you have a permit for that gun, Scarlet?" Kate asked.

"Darling, I don't need a permit. I was in the OSS. I have a pass."

"They don't hand out passes to carry weapons because you slept with Nazis seventy years ago."

"I've always liked you, Kate," Scarlet said with a smile. "Let me give you some advice. Germans are terrible in bed. Avoid them at all costs. But if you want to get them to talk, just stick your finger straight up their butthole. Works every time."

Scarlet looked around the room and wandered to Kate's desk, picking up the candy dish of Hershey's Kisses and sticking the entire thing into her purse.

"I'm married," Kate said dryly. "He's Scottish."

"Well, maybe you can do better next time, dearie. I enjoyed my fourth husband immensely."

Scarlet poured herself a cup of coffee and helped herself to one of the cinnamon rolls before sitting in the chair Kate normally occupied during meetings.

"Sit, girls. Time is of the essence here. I could die tomorrow."

I shrugged and freshened my coffee and got a new cup for Kate as well. Kate and I had been friends forever, but sometimes I was a trial. And that included stray family members that had popped in and out of my life through the years.

"Does Mom know you're in town?" I asked, taking my usual spot on the sofa next to Kate.

"Heavens no. And we're going to keep this our little secret. Your mother is always trying to steal my thunder. There can only be one eccentric in a family and until I die that's me."

Though Scarlet had been married five times, she'd stopped changing her name after her second husband because she hated the lines at the social security office. She'd said she was born Scarlet Holmes and that's how she wanted to die.

"I thought you were living on one of those cruise ships," Kate said.

Scarlet waved the statement away and took a bite of the cinnamon roll. She was a Holmes all right. I got that same look on my face whenever eating sweets or having an orgasm.

"That ended after Thanksgiving. I think the captain was drugging me and sneaking into my room at night to fondle me. I woke up every morning with a horrible hangover and no underwear. He tried to tell me it was because I was drinking too much and leaving my underpants on the craps table for good luck, but that's ridiculous. I don't even play craps. Everyone knows that roulette is my game."

A horrible thought struck me and I blurted out, "Are you moving back to Whiskey Bayou?"

"Hell no," she said, appalled. "Lord, I hate that place. Though I like to go and visit the cemetery because I know everyone buried there. It's a lot easier to talk to people when they don't have the capability of talking back."

She let out a gentle belch and then leaned back and propped her sneakered feet on the table.

"After the cruise ship I found a little resort place in Florida. It's always warm and it's right on the water. I can't wait to get back. This cold is terrible on my bones. Can't even feel my nipples. I smashed one of them in the car door and didn't even notice."

"You drove here?" I asked, unsuccessful at keeping the terror out of my voice.

"You bet. Just bought a brand new Hummer. It's a real beaut. You don't even notice when you run over things."

"Christ," Kate said under her breath.

"How long are you staying?" I asked.

"That's what I'm trying to explain. We need to get back there lickety-split."

"We?" Kate and I said together.

"You girls don't have the sense that God gave a goose. I'm trying to tell you something important here. I've found a murderer!"

Read more of the story here!
Whiskey on the Rocks

ABOUT THE AUTHOR

Liliana Hart is a *New York Times*, *USA Today*, and Publisher's Weekly bestselling author of more than sixty titles. After starting her first novel her freshman year of college, she immediately became addicted to writing and knew she'd found what she was meant to do with her life. She has no idea why she majored in music.

Since publishing in June 2011, Liliana has sold more than six-million books. All three of her series have made multiple appearances on the *New York Times* list.

Liliana can almost always be found at her

computer writing, hauling five kids to various activities, or spending time with her husband. She calls Texas home.

If you enjoyed reading this, I would appreciate it if you would help others enjoy this book, too.

Recommend it. Please help other readers find this book by recommending it to friends, readers' groups and discussion boards.

Review it. Please tell other readers why you liked this book by reviewing.

Connect with me online:
www.lilianahart.com

facebook.com/LilianaHart

instagram.com/LilianaHart

bookbub.com/authors/liliana-hart

ALSO BY LILIANA HART

JJ Graves Mystery Series

Dirty Little Secrets

A Dirty Shame

Dirty Rotten Scoundrel

Down and Dirty

Dirty Deeds

Dirty Laundry

Dirty Money

A Dirty Job

Dirty Devil

Playing Dirty

Dirty Martini

Addison Holmes Mystery Series

Whiskey Rebellion

Whiskey Sour

Whiskey For Breakfast

Whiskey, You're The Devil

Whiskey on the Rocks

Whiskey Tango Foxtrot

Whiskey and Gunpowder

Whiskey Lullaby

The Scarlet Chronicles

Bouncing Betty

Hand Grenade Helen

Front Line Francis

The Harley and Davidson Mystery Series

The Farmer's Slaughter

A Tisket a Casket

I Saw Mommy Killing Santa Claus

Get Your Murder Running

Deceased and Desist

Malice in Wonderland

Tequila Mockingbird

Gone With the Sin

Grime and Punishment

Blazing Rattles

A Salt and Battery

Curl Up and Dye

First Comes Death Then Comes Marriage

Box Set 1

Box Set 2

Box Set 3

The Gravediggers

The Darkest Corner

Gone to Dust

Say No More